"Why didn't you tell me about the baby?" Dawson asked.

"I was scared."

He shot her a look.

"Why didn't you really?"

She shrugged.

"What aren't you telling me?" he demanded.

"It's going to take time to learn everything about him, Dawson," she hedged, trying to redirect the conversation back to a comfortable place. "Maybe it's enough for the two of you to get to know each other. We don't have to do this all in one day, do we?"

"No. Of course not. But I have every intention of being there for my son as he grows up."

TEXAN'S BABY

USA TODAY Bestselling Author
BARB HAN

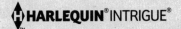

I owe a debt of gratitude to Allison Lyons and Jill Marsal for the chance
to work with you both, the best editor and agent in the business.
Thank you to the entire team at Harlequin Intrigue, led by Denise Zaza,
for brilliant editorial, art and marketing. I'm blown away every time.

There are a few people who inspire me, breathing joy and laughter
into every day...Brandon, Jacob and Tori; I hope you know
how much I love you. And to John, my one great love,
for being the person I can't wait to talk to at the end of each day.

A huge thank-you to Chrissy McDowell for her medical research help
and to her daughter, Morgan, for her all-around awesomeness
and bright red hair.

ISBN-13: 978-0-373-69900-1

PLEASE RECYCLE

THIS PRODUCT IS RECYCLABLE

Texan's Baby

Recycling programs
for this product may
not exist in your area.

HARLEQUIN®

www.Harlequin.com

Printed in U.S.A.

USA TODAY bestselling author **Barb Han** lives in north Texas with her very own hero-worthy husband, three beautiful children, a spunky golden retriever/standard poodle mix and too many books in her to-read pile. In her downtime, she plays video games and spends much of her time on or around a basketball court. She loves interacting with readers and is grateful for their support. You can reach her at barbhan.com.

Books by Barb Han

Harlequin Intrigue

Mason Ridge

Texas Prey
Texas Takedown
Texas Hunt
Texan's Baby

The Campbells of Creek Bend

Witness Protection
Gut Instinct
Hard Target

Rancher Rescue

Harlequin Intrigue Noir

Atomic Beauty

CAST OF CHARACTERS

Melanie Dixon—The secret she's been keeping from Dawson Hill is about to be exposed just as a stalker from her past sets his sights on her.

Dawson Hill—Losing his little sister so early in life to a terrible and rare disease is something he never recovered from. Melanie pulled him back from the depths all those years ago and was his best friend until she cut off contact and disappeared after their friendship turned romantic. Now that she's being stalked, he'll have to come to terms with his past and face his own fears in order to ensure her safety. Can he save her in time?

Mason Hill—The son Dawson didn't know existed.

Bethany Hill—The little sister whose death forever haunts Dawson.

Beckett Alcorn—While in jail, he gave up his partner, Jordan Sprigs, in exchange for leniency.

Jordan Sprigs—He's been obsessed with Melanie for years. Now that he's wanted in connection with a criminal child abduction ring, he has nothing to lose.

Chapter One

Dawson Hill stared at the two-story Folk Victorian across the street intently. It was two o'clock in the morning and he'd been in the same spot at the front window an embarrassing number of hours already. He was staying the night at his childhood home in hopes that he would figure out a good reason to approach her. If he thought he could get a straight answer out of Melanie Dixon, he'd stalk over and ask her outright. As it was, he could only guess why she'd disappeared two and a half years ago, not long after they'd started what he thought was a real relationship. Normally he'd be able to let it go and not look back, but they'd known each other since they were kids and it wasn't like her to pull such a stunt.

Movement across the street caught Dawson's eye. A dark silhouette crossed the front window. Was someone on her porch? Why would anyone be moving around outside in the dark at this time of night? The thought sat in his gut about as well as eating a handful of nails.

Beckett Alcorn, aka The Mason Ridge Abductor—the most notorious criminal in Mason Ridge's history—was in jail where he belonged. That should have ended the terror that had haunted this town for fifteen years. Except that, in return for leniency, Alcorn gave up his partner's name. He and Jordan Sprigs had been running a child abduction ring throughout Texas for the past fifteen years. Sprigs was believed to be out of the state, in hiding.

The town should be able to rest easy. It couldn't. The feds had been brought in to actively look for Sprigs. This was the last place anyone expected to find him. And yet no one felt safe. This case never seemed to close. Maybe that was the reason Dawson didn't believe it was over, either.

Now that Alcorn was behind bars and every available law enforcement officer was seeking Sprigs, the town was supposed to be able to move forward. Go back to their normal lives. And yet little things were still going bump in the night. Or in this case, shadows were moving across windows.

Melanie's parents were on the road, so Dawson already knew she was home alone. Her parents had spent every summer in their RV traveling around the US since retiring from the post office half a dozen years ago.

Because she was by herself in the house and Dawson's creepy radar was on full alert, he slipped out the back door to investigate.

A quick walk around the perimeter followed by peeking in a couple of windows just to make sure she wasn't in trouble would allow him to rest peacefully. Rest? He suppressed a laugh. Knowing Melanie was across the street alone while one of Mason Ridge's most notorious criminals was on the loose wasn't exactly the cure for insomnia.

Making sure she was safe would go a long way toward giving him the peace of mind he needed to sleep, he told himself. And this had nothing to do with the fact that he needed to see her again.

Dawson ignored the little voice in the back of his mind calling him a liar and slipped across the street.

With every step toward Melanie's place, the hair on Dawson's neck pricked. What was that all about? He didn't believe in the hype about black cats walking over graves or bad luck following walking under a ladder. He believed what was right in front of his nose. If he could see, touch or hear it, then it existed.

The front curtain moved as he positioned himself inside the Japanese boxwoods lining the perimeter to gain a better view over the porch. Whatever was on the other side of the wall five feet away had his senses screeching on full alert. The sirens in his head were so loud he'd have one helluva headache if he didn't silence them soon.

Climbing onto the wraparound porch, he listened carefully. The inside of the house was pitch-black, and there was no sound of breaking lamps or noises associated with stumbling into chairs or side tables. Whoever was in there most likely knew the layout. This was knowledge Melanie would have, but why would she creep around in her childhood house in the dark? Didn't make any sense, which was another reason the warning bells inside his head were ringing so loud his ears hurt.

If he covered all the possible scenarios, then he had to consider the notion that she had a boyfriend. There could be a guy in there trying not to wake her.

Dawson glanced over at the carport. All he saw was Melanie's vehicle, which revealed nothing. She could've picked the guy up in order to keep their relationship under wraps.

Thinking about Melanie with another man didn't do good things to Dawson's blood pressure. And yet he had no right to be angry.

There were other possibilities. Melanie had a sister, Abby. Dawson was sure he'd seen her around town yesterday, but he'd assumed that she'd gone back to Austin when her car disappeared last night.

The RV was gone, so there was no chance her parents had returned.

An ugly thought struck. Was Dawson making an excuse to spy on her? Had he really seen what he thought or was his mind playing tricks on him? He quickly dismissed the notion. Even though she'd been more frigid than crab fishermen's waters since their breakup—if he could call it that—he needed to make sure she was safe, especially while Sprigs was still free. Their mutual friend Lisa was still recovering from being attacked in connection with this case.

Dawson peeked through the front window. He couldn't see a thing.

How many hours had he spent inside that house as a kid?

How many since? He and Melanie had started things up between them when she took a job as a paralegal a couple years after she'd graduated from college. Things were going well until she'd abruptly told him it was over and then pulled a Houdini, moving to Houston and cutting off all contact. Said she'd moved on and had meant it literally and figuratively. Her stuff had disappeared from her parents' place where she'd been staying, and she hadn't taken his calls since. Didn't he lick a few wounds over that?

The time or two he'd been drunk enough to torture himself by looking at a picture of her online hadn't given him any more of a clue as to what he'd done wrong. Her privacy settings on her social media pages were set tighter than perimeter patrol at Leavenworth, so he couldn't see much beyond her profile picture.

Dawson slipped around back of the house and onto the screened porch. He'd remind her to keep that locked the next time he saw her. Yeah, he'd be the first one she'd want to talk to. She'd been home four days already and had managed to avoid talking to him so far. Since they shared the same friends, that took effort.

A shadow moved in the hallway toward the kitchen. Based on the size of this one, Dawson assumed it belonged to a male. Shadows could be deceiving.

The figure retreated. Dawson crouched low to make himself as small as possible—which was difficult given his six-foot-three frame—in case the dark figure returned. His eyes had adjusted to the darkness and there was just enough light coming off the appliances to see the kitchen fairly well.

Years ago, the Dixons used to hide a key in a fake rock near the porch. He dropped down to the bottom of the stairs now and felt around. Bingo.

Dawson slipped the key in the lock and then froze. If memory served, the Dixons had had an alarm installed for when they went on long road trips. He had an auxiliary code for emergencies, so he was good there. His grip tightened around the door knob.

Hold on a second.

If the door chime was on, he'd be given up the second he opened that door. He muttered a curse.

The telltale double click of a shotgun engaging a shell in the chamber sounded from behind.

Dawson spun around and stared at Melanie.

"Put that thing away before you hurt me." He waved her off.

"What are you doing here, Dawson Hill?" She studied him intently. Her legs were apart, positioned in an athletic stance, and the determination on her face said she'd shoot if she had to. She had the feral disposition of a mama bear protecting her cubs.

"Hold on there." Dawson's hands came up in surrender.

"Why don't you lower that thing before you accidentally pull the trigger?"

She dropped the barrel, allowing it to rest on her forearm. It was the easiest spot to pull up and shoot from, Dawson noted.

"You didn't answer my question," she said, a look of sheer panic in her eyes. And there was another emotion present that Dawson couldn't quite put his finger on, but it was intense.

"Trying to make sure no one's breaking into your parents' house." His hands still in the air, he stared at her. Damn, she looked good. It was too dark to see all the flecks in her honey-brown eyes, but she still had that dancer's body she'd earned at Nina's Dance Studio in town. Her hips had filled out in the sexiest curves. The silhouette of her long, wavy blond hair said she'd let it grow out since he'd last seen her. He flexed his fingers to distract himself from wanting to reach out to touch her smooth glowing skin and he wondered if she would still quiver if he ran his hand along the lines of her flat stomach.

Given the fact that a shotgun barrel was pointed right at his groin, his thoughts couldn't be more inappropriate. Dawson sidestepped the line of the barrel.

"What makes you think someone's trying to get in here?" The edge to her voice was another slap of reality.

It was clear that she'd rather face down a robber than see Dawson again. Now, wasn't that interesting? Apparently she regretted the time they'd spent together, especially given the way she'd bolted without a word not long after. Personally, he thought the sex had ranked right up there with the best he'd ever had.

Since Dawson didn't want to admit he'd been staring out the window half the night just to catch a glimpse of her, he decided to say, "Woke to a noise across the street and followed it here."

She gave him a quick once-over, her disbelief written all over her expression.

Yeah, he was still fully dressed. She would know that he slept in boxers and nothing else.

Her gaze narrowed as she took him in. "Looks like you just woke up all right. And I'm the tooth fairy."

"That's good to know, because I've been meaning to talk to you about that nickel you left me in second grade." Normally a statement like that would make her smile and then she'd fire a snappy comeback at him. He'd always loved her sense of humor. She wasn't buying in this time. Her glare could crack ice.

"No one's here but me and you. *You* should go." Didn't her tone just send an icy shiver down his back? Who needed air-conditioning with the chill she put in the air?

He needed to man up and ask her what was really on his mind while he had her here. He couldn't pinpoint the reason, maybe it was her mood, but he decided not to push his luck. In her state of mind she might just tell him. Brutal honesty could be the most painful kind, and a small part of him—the part that still had feelings for her—didn't want to know.

"Just as soon as I know you're okay." He took a step toward her. "And you put that shotgun away."

"You're looking at me. Do I seem fine to you?"

He wasn't about to touch that statement. "Let me double-check the place to be sure. I saw someone moving around inside. I won't be able to go back to sleep until I know you're safe."

Her cocked eyebrow and the way she looked him up and down again said he needed to drop the act. They both knew he wasn't asleep before.

"I can handle myself, Dawson. I don't need your help."

Most women would balk at the idea of going inside a house alone if there could be an intruder present. Melanie had always been able to stick up for herself, but she'd never been foolish. What was going on? Did she hate him so much that she'd be willing to risk her own safety just so she wouldn't have to look at him again?

"Then do it for me," he said.

"I already told you no." She moved around to block his access to the door, her back to the kitchen.

If he didn't know her any better, he'd say she was hiding something...or someone.

Reality hit him hard. She wasn't alone.

The last thing Dawson needed to see was the other guy. That would be an image he'd never be able to erase. It would burn into his retinas and his heart. "Suit yourself."

He turned and took a step toward the screen door.

A noise pierced the awkward silence. Then a sudden burst exploded behind him and he turned in time to see a little kid, bawling, running toward Melanie.

What the hell?

The kid had to be at least a year, maybe two. His friend Dylan's daughter was three and she looked much older than this guy.

Melanie swore under her breath, loud enough that Dawson heard but quiet enough to shield the kid.

The little boy moved closer, into the light, and Dawson's jaw fell slack.

Staring up at him was the spitting image *of him*.

Chapter Two

Melanie's pulse raced, her heart hammering on her rib cage as she started toward her son. *This cannot be happening.*

Her entire world was crashing down around her and it was hard to breathe. One look at Dawson and it was clear that he'd put two and two together. Her secret was out in the open.

She examined Dawson's reaction as panic welled inside her.

Pure unadulterated anger fired through his eyes when he glared at her. Melanie placed the shotgun on the cushion of the wicker sofa as she raced toward her son, who was crying and still half-asleep, with her arms open. "It's okay, baby."

"We're going to talk," Dawson said in a low growl that sent a chill racing down her spine.

Returning to Mason Ridge had been the worst of bad ideas.

This wasn't how things were supposed to go down. Abby had been supposed to stay in Houston with Mason, not bring him back to Mason Ridge. Her sister had called saying that Mason wouldn't stop crying and that his forehead felt warm. Even after Melanie had reassured her sister that he was most likely cutting teeth and would be fine, Abby had insisted she come anyway. She'd shown up four hours later.

Fear had gripped Melanie when she thought about Dawson's parents living right across the street and possibly seeing her son. Dawson visited all the time. He was too close, and her worst-case scenario was playing out all around her as she hugged her son closer to her chest and consoled him.

The heat of Dawson's glare practically burned holes through the back of her head. She didn't need to turn around to know he was staring at her. The only surprise was that he'd been mute so far. That scared her the most.

She felt Mason's forehead and frowned.

"He's burning up. I need to take him inside. You already know the way out."

"Nice try, but I'm not leaving until we talk." His tone was lighter than she expected and she quickly realized he wouldn't want to scare the baby. At least that would buy her some goodwill.

She exhaled.

"Fine." She patted Mason's back and he felt warm there, too. He hiccupped and coughed, and his chest sounded croupy.

Dawson followed her inside. His silence was worse than any words he could've thrown at her. She'd almost rather he yell. The guilt that had been eating at her insides for months was about to destroy her stomach lining.

No. She wouldn't do this to herself again. She'd made the right call, she reminded herself, the *only* one she could've made under the circumstances and especially after the warning from Dawson's mother.

And yet Melanie couldn't shake the feeling that everything was crumbling around her.

"Can you get a clean washcloth from the linen closet

down the hall and wet it?" She couldn't worry about Dawson right now. Mason was her priority. She carried her clinging eighteen-month-old son to the couch. He was dead weight in her arms, already in the ninety-seventh percentile for height and weight, and she felt every one of his twenty-six pounds.

Dawson disappeared down the hall, returning a few moments later with the offering. His dark brow creased with worry. He could be intimidating with his tall and powerful frame, and pitch-black hair. He had the face of a warrior…long, strong chin, hawk nose and serious dark brown eyes. But she'd seen the softer side to Dawson and knew exactly where her son got his kind disposition.

Dawson sat on the edge of the solid wood block coffee table.

Normally shy, Mason didn't blink twice at the stranger's presence. But then Dawson wasn't exactly a random person. He was Mason's father. Did her son know that somehow?

A fresh wave of guilt washed over her as she took the wet cloth from Dawson and placed it on her son's forehead.

"Stay right here, baby. Mommy's going to get you some medicine."

"Who's dat, Mama?" came out through a yawn. His normally bright dark eyes were glossy and dull from fever. This was more than teething and Melanie was glad Abby hadn't listened earlier.

"Mr. Hill is a nice man." She risked a glance at Dawson, who hadn't stopped staring at their son. No way could she get him to leave now, not with all those questions brewing behind those dark eyes. "He's going to help us tonight. Okay?"

Mason nodded and then closed his red-rimmed eyes.

"I'll be right back, sweetie."

She returned with a fever-reducing medicine strip that would melt on Mason's tongue as soon as he opened his mouth.

Dawson's body was square with her son, he was leaning forward, and he seemed protective of the little boy already. Melanie couldn't deny how right it felt to see the two of them together, no matter how much the thought she could lose Mason caused her chest to tighten.

When she got close enough, she could see that Dawson was holding Mason's hand. Her heart skipped a beat.

Nothing was ever going to be the same again.

Right now the only thing that mattered was getting Mason's fever down. She'd have to deal with the rest later.

"Open up, baby," she said.

Mason did. He'd always been an easy child.

She placed the small strip on his tongue. "Fifteen minutes and you'll feel all better."

He yawned again and rubbed his eyes. "Sleepy."

"Try to rest." She couldn't help noticing that Dawson still held her son's hand.

Melanie perched on the couch next to Mason, turning the cloth to the cooler side, rubbing his back.

"What's going on with him?" Dawson whispered. Concern deepened his tone.

"At first I thought he was teething but it has to be more." All of Dawson's attention was on Mason. Good. Melanie wouldn't be able to stand it if Dawson scrutinized her."He's had teething syndrome, which means several of his teeth have been trying to come in at the same time. They've been giving him fits."

"But that doesn't explain the coughing and congestion."

"Exactly."

He looked up at her. Sensual heat crawled up her neck,

and her face heated, which couldn't be more unwelcome under the circumstances. She diverted her eyes to Mason, her safe place. No one could argue she'd been a good mother. Well, no one but her. Apparently delivering a child meant second-guessing every decision. By the time Mason's first birthday rolled around, she realized it was most likely a normal part of the turf.

Growing up watching her own parents live in a loveless marriage, Melanie didn't want to make the same mistakes. She wondered if they'd ever really been in love. Their relationship felt more as if they existed in the same house, like roommates and not husband and wife.

What they had was more of a mutual understanding than a marriage, and maybe a healthy fear of ending up alone.

If Melanie committed herself to a man, she wanted fire and spark and forever. Not someone content to live under the same roof or who was afraid to be by themselves.

And maybe that was a childish notion. Until she was sure about a relationship, she had no problem going solo. But then her last relationship, the one with Dawson, had set the bar pretty high before the unexpected pregnancy and everything that followed.

Fifteen minutes had passed and Mason's skin was beginning to cool. He'd turned on his side and his breathing had grown steady. Sleep was a good thing for her little angel.

Dawson pulled his cell out of his pocket.

"Who are you calling in the middle of the night?" she whispered.

"My mother. She'll know what to do." His voice was low.

She's already done enough, Melanie thought.

"It's too late," she said with a little too much emotion. "And this isn't the first routine fever I've gotten my son through."

"Is it? *Routine*?" The way he emphasized that last word made her realize he had other questions about his son's health, questions she knew would come.

"It's already coming down." Panic skittered across her nerves. His mother's words wound through Melanie's thoughts. If the baby became sick from the genetic illness that had taken his baby sister far too early, Dawson wouldn't survive. Then she'd reminded Melanie that Dawson had been adamant about never having kids of his own. He would never risk putting a child through the same thing his sister had endured. His mother had said that if Melanie told him about the baby, then he'd stick around, trapped, and that he'd resent her for the rest of their lives.

Melanie thought about her parents, who'd been forced to marry after an unplanned pregnancy, about their empty lives.

"He felt so hot when I touched his forehead. He was an inferno. It can't hurt to get a doctor's opinion," Dawson said, forcing her out of deep thought.

"Mason tends to get sick fast and hard, and he gets the worst temps. Luckily, he gets over them just as quickly. He needs rest and plenty of fluids. I'll give his pediatrician a call in the morning just to be sure."

"His name is Mason." It was more statement than question, the fire still burning behind Dawson's eyes.

"Yes."

"How did this happen?" He held up his free hand. "Don't answer that…*that* I know."

Her cheeks flamed.

"The rest is complicated." Her gaze bounced from Dawson to Mason. She didn't want to disturb his peaceful sleep.

"Not from my viewpoint." Frustration and confusion drew his dark eyebrows together.

"I'm exhausted, Dawson. I've been worried about Mason. Is there any chance we can talk about this tomorrow?" She started to turn but was stopped by his strong hand on her arm. She ignored the sensual trill vibrating through her where he touched, shrugging out of his grip.

"I saw a shadow pass by the front window. I should investigate before I leave. Besides, I'm not going anywhere until I know why this is the first time I found out I have a son." His voice carried a subtle threat, but there was no way Dawson would ever act on it. He was hurt, she could see that in his eyes, and he needed time to adjust to this new reality.

"Do we have to go through this right now?" she asked, hoping for more time, time to clear up her churning thoughts so she could speak like a reasonable adult.

The look he shot her could've burned a hole in Sheetrock. "Don't you think you've kept him from me long enough? Or that he deserves to know he has a father?"

"He needs his rest and I don't want to disturb him. We can talk tomorrow," she said as coldly as she could manage with Dawson so close.

"Oh, you really must think I'm an idiot. First, you hide my own son from me for...how old is he?"

"Eighteen months."

"A full year and a half...and then you think you can just tell me to leave so you can slip out of town again. Not this time. I'm not leaving your side until I know everything."

Hell would freeze over before she'd tell him the whole truth. Besides, he was acting as if this were all her fault and that fired anger through her veins. She wasn't just being selfish by not telling him about Mason, she'd been trying to protect him. "It takes two to tango, mister. You had to know this was a possibility."

"But we were careful."

"Condoms are only effective 98 percent of the time. Look who's in the 2 percent." She held her hands up and shrugged.

"They really should put that on the package." His anger was still rumbling along the surface and this was not the time for a rational discussion.

"They do. You'd need a magnifying glass to find it. At least, that's what I used." Her attempt at humor was met with a chilly response. For a split second, she wished for that carefree breezy smile of Dawson's. The way one of his lips curled in a half smile was just about the sexiest thing she'd seen. And it had been great at seducing her. Just thinking about it caused a similar reaction she had to consciously shut down.

She refocused on a sigh. "You already know he's eighteen months, so ask me something else."

"How'd you decide on his name?"

"It was easy. That's where he was conceived." She didn't want to admit to Dawson how very special that day was to her. And it had been.

"The night we spent at Mason Ridge Lake?"

She nodded. Dawson deserved to know that much at least. She had no plans to tell him what had happened a few weeks afterward in his mother's office. Her shoulders relaxed a bit the way they always did when she talked about her son, correction, *their* son. Like it or not, Dawson was most likely going to be part of their lives. For Mason's sake, that was a good thing. But she was worried about Dawson. Had she just condemned him to the fate she'd most feared? "What else do you want to know?"

"I don't even know where to start." Bewildered, he

rubbed the scruff on his chin. "What kinds of toys does he like?"

"The usual stuff babies like. Balls, trucks and baby dolls."

"You let him play with—"

"Don't even say it." She shot him a look that scolded him without another word.

"No. You're right. That was stupid and sexist of me." He paused. "You're sure he's going to be okay? He's so little and seems so...fragile."

The look on Dawson's face spoke volumes about how afraid he was for Mason. Of course, he wouldn't say that if he had to lug the little bugger around all day. But that wasn't really the question he was asking.

As far as Melanie knew, their son was fine. But then, the disease Dawson worried about wouldn't show up until later. There was genetic testing available but Melanie had been too freaked out to take that step. She would. There'd come a point in the near future when she would need to know. Up until now, she'd been able to bury the thought down deep.

"He's strong and healthy," she said for both of their benefits. "His fevers always scare the heck out of me, but he should be good by tomorrow. It's probably a virus and that's the reason for the cough."

"Sounds worse than that." Dawson stuffed his cell into his pocket. "If you won't let me call my mother, then we should take him to the emergency room or something. Mercy's open."

"He needs rest for now." She positioned extra pillows around his sides so he wouldn't roll off the sofa. If she were going to have this conversation or any conversation with Dawson she needed caffeine.

She moved to the fridge, Dawson on her heels, and

pulled out a Pepsi. Normally, she fixed a glass with ice and a lime wedge, but this situation called for emergency measures. The cap was off and she'd had her first swallow before Dawson could fire another question.

"Where do the two of you live?" His face was stone and she had no idea what he was thinking.

"Outside of Houston. We have a two-bedroom apartment there in a suburb."

"What about work? What do you do for a living?"

She didn't want to tell him. He'd judge her. Maybe even call her an unfit mother. Oh, no, would he try to take Mason away from her? Courts might side with him, given that she'd kept their little boy a secret all these months— a fact that she hadn't thought about until now. His family had enough money to wage war if they wanted to. Panic washed over her in a tidal wave mixed with other emotions. All her fears pressed down on her like concrete slabs pulling her to the bottom of the ocean. She put her hand to her chest.

"Breathe." That one word, spoken with authority, was more calming than it should be.

"I need to check on Mason." She took her Pepsi into the living room where she could keep an eye on her son.

Dawson followed.

"Let's sit over here so we can talk and keep an eye on him," she said, pointing to the pair of wingback chairs nestled near the fireplace as she eyed Dawson wearily, praying the caffeine would kick in.

"I'm not going to try to steal him, so you can stop looking at me like that," Dawson said.

"You want coffee or something?" She'd rehearsed this scenario inside her mind a thousand times. Facing him, seeing the hurt in his eyes planted so much doubt about her actions up until now.

"No, thanks. I'll take a Pepsi, though."

She retrieved another bottle and handed it to him as they returned to the wingback chairs near Mason.

Here goes.

Melanie opened her mouth to speak and then clamped it shut. A noise in the other room stopped her cold. "Did you hear that?"

"Get the baby and get ready to run on my word. Don't wait for me to come back. Just go when I say." Dawson was already on his feet, moving toward the kitchen so stealthily with his back against the wall that his movement almost didn't register.

By the second noise, Mason was in her arms and an ominous feeling had settled over her. Her purse was on the foyer table next to the front door, keys inside.

She heard a scuffle and then Dawson shouted, "Go!"

Her need to protect her son warred with her desire to make sure his father was okay.

Dawson had told her to leave.

She dug out her keys from the bottom of her bag, hands shaking, praying Mason would stay asleep on her shoulder.

As she stepped onto the front porch, a shotgun blasted in the other room.

Chapter Three

Melanie's pulse raced as Mason opened his eyes and bawled so loudly there was no covering it. The sound would alert whoever had the gun, and chances were that person wasn't Dawson. A knife pierced her chest at the thought of him being shot, bleeding. She had very much loved him and the two had been inseparable for most of their childhoods.

She bolted across the porch and down the stairs.

Mason wriggled, working up to release another round.

"It's okay, baby," she soothed as she made a run for her car, her legs bogged down by what felt like lead weights as she thought about leaving Dawson behind.

The carport on the side of the house was equal distance from the front and back doors. Anything happened to Dawson—and she prayed that wasn't the case—and the attacker could get to her and Mason easily.

She couldn't allow herself to think that anything could happen to Dawson, no matter how heavy her heart was in her chest, trying to convince her otherwise.

The auto unlock caused her sedan's lights to blink and make a clicking sound. Mason stirred and she feared he was about to wail again giving away their location, but he whimpered instead.

Melanie repeated a protection prayer she'd learned as

a child as she tucked Mason into the car seat. She half expected someone to come up from behind and jerk her away from her son. Or another sudden blast to split the air.

No matter how torn she felt between running to safety with her Mason and staying back to help his father, she would go. Dawson had ordered her to take the baby and run, and she had to believe—no, pray—he knew what he was doing.

Getting the key in the ignition was difficult with shaky hands. Adrenaline had kicked in and her insides churned. She finally managed on her fourth attempt. Mason stirred, crying louder, winding up to release a scream. The energy he was expending threw him into another coughing fit. And there was nothing she could do about it, which sent her stress hormones soaring.

Melanie backed out of the carport with blacked-out lights. She turned the car around so that she could better see as she navigated the gravel driveway.

With the windows up Mason's crying would be muffled to anyone outside the car. Leaving him in the backseat, not being able to comfort him while he cried ripped out another piece of her heart. As soon as she could be sure she'd gotten them out of there and to safety, she'd pull over. No, she'd call 9-1-1 first.

Nearing the end of the driveway, she was almost to the street when a dark figure jumped in front of the car.

Melanie slammed on the brakes and flipped on her headlights.

It was Dawson…covered in blood.

She unlocked the doors, motioning for him to get inside while scanning the darkness for his attacker. Her heart sank. She could get him to Mercy Hospital in twenty minutes.

He darted to the passenger side, opened the door and jumped in. "Go."

No other word was needed. As soon as his door closed, she gunned it, spinning out in the gravel. She eased her foot off the gas pedal enough for the tires to gain traction, cut a right at the end of the drive and sped toward Mercy.

"Dawson, you're shot."

"It's not that bad," he said.

Mason's cries intensified. She glanced in the rearview and saw that his eyes were closed as he tried to shove his fist in his mouth.

"You have blood all over you," she said to Dawson, not masking the panic in her voice as her heart ached to hold her son.

"It looks worse than it is," he said, dismissing her concern and focusing on Mason. "What can I do to help him?"

"There's an emergency pacifier in the diaper bag in the floorboard." She motioned toward the backseat. "I've been weaning him."

Dawson held up his bloody hands.

"There are wet wipes in the bag, too."

Dawson grunted in pain as he twisted around and pulled wipes from the bag. Distress was stamped all over his features at hearing the baby cry.

Melanie had had the same look when her son was born and she realized that she didn't have the first idea how to take care of a baby. A few months later, she'd become an old hand at caring for Mason, and she had no doubt that Dawson would, too.

As soon as the pacifier was in Mason's mouth, he quieted.

"Make a left at the next light," Dawson said, sounding satisfied.

She remembered that feeling well. Those early wins were important confidence boosters.

"You're hurt. I'm taking you to the hospital," she said emphatically.

"No. I'm fine." There was no room for argument in his tone. "A piece of the slug grazed my shoulder. That's all."

"It looks a lot worse than that," she said. Was he down-playing his injury? She wanted to believe he was fine. From her periphery she saw him one-arm his shirt off and then roll it up.

"Nah. I'll be okay."

"I have a medical kit in the glove box. There are a few supplies in there that should help."

"Since when did you start keeping an emergency kit in your car?" he asked.

"Mason was climbing up the stairs to a slide at a playground. A mom asked me a question, distracted me for one second. I looked away. Next thing I know, Mason's screaming and blood's pouring from his forehead. A nice couple brought over a few supplies they'd learned to keep with them. I made my own kit after that."

"The sound of his crying is heartbreaking. He's quiet, but what if he loses that pacifier I put in his mouth? Should I go back there and hold him or something?"

"Not with blood all over you. Plus, he's safer in his car seat."

"You're right. Of course. I don't know how you can listen to him and still drive. It kills me," he admitted.

"Believe me, it isn't easy." She didn't want to say that she'd had more practice than Dawson or remind him of what he'd already missed.

"I'll watch out to make sure we're not being followed," he said.

"Who was it back there?" she asked. "Did you get a good look at him?"

"I didn't recognize the guy. We had a scuffle and he got hold of the shotgun. He pulled the trigger as he ran away."

"I thought for sure it would be Sprigs." Relief flooded her that it wasn't him.

"What would he want with you?"

"He's always given me the creeps," she said with a shiver.

"Ever since he developed that crush on you when you were in middle school and couldn't let it go?"

"Yes. And every few months he felt the need to make sure I knew he still liked me. He was really upset when you and I started dating and sent me a few odd messages through social media. I tightened all my privacy controls when I left town so he couldn't see any of my stuff. I hoped that would send him the message to leave me alone." Learning he was involved in a child abduction ring had shocked her until she really thought about it. Sprigs was creepy before. Now he was flat-out dangerous.

"Why didn't you tell me?" he asked.

"Had no reason to before. I just thought he was a creep. Now, with everything going on I'm scared."

"What makes you think it might've been him tonight?" Dawson asked.

"I'm pretty sure that I got a piece of mail from him at my parent's house the other day. It was cryptic but alluded to the fact that we'd be together again someday. At the time, I thought he might be saying good-bye."

"And now you're worried he means you'll be together now," Dawson said through what sounded like clenched teeth.

She gripped the steering wheel tighter.

Mason stirred, crying without opening his eyes.

Melanie sang her son's favorite song while Dawson worked on his flesh wound for the rest of the ride. The baby settled halfway through the lyrics and fell back into a deep sleep.

Riding in a car helped. How many times had she driven around the block to get him to take a nap in the past year and a half? She'd lost count.

Singing in front of Dawson should embarrass her. For some reason, it didn't. She chalked it up to their history and tried not to read anything more into it.

It would be nice to know what Dawson was thinking. Then again, after all that had happened tonight, maybe not knowing was better.

Reporting the crime didn't take long. The deputy said he'd check the house personally and then lock up using the spare key Dawson provided. He also said that he'd make a note on the Sprigs case about the letter even though he seemed unconvinced the two were related, stating that stalkers acted alone.

"That seemed like a waste of time," Melanie said to Dawson on the way out of the sheriff's office.

"Agreed. Burglaries do happen, but this was not one of them. I have a feeling you're right about Sprigs and he's behind this in some way."

"Like I told the deputy, I'm not going back to that house tonight and I don't for one minute believe that could be random," Melanie said, patting Mason's back as he slept with his head on her shoulder.

Dawson agreed. "We're not staying at my parents' place, either. Sprigs is still on the loose and our friends have been targeted before. We need to take every precaution necessary to ensure your safety."

She wasn't sure she liked the sound of "we." However, she wasn't in a position to argue.

"That's part of the reason I was watching your house earlier." He seemed to realize that he hadn't meant to share that news, giving an awkward glance in her direction. "I was concerned about you, Melanie, and it wasn't like you were talking to me."

"I'm glad you were there, no matter what the actual reason was."

"By the looks of your initial reaction to my presence, you can take care of yourself." His tone was lighter and that was meant to be a joke.

It should be funny.

Being a single parent was more than difficult, even though Melanie wouldn't trade one single day with Mason for the world. If she were being totally honest, though, she was tired of taking care of everything on her own. Or maybe she was just tired. The early months had been a string of missed nights of sleep. Taking care of her son alone had been tough and rewarding and exhausting.

And lonely.

Part of her had a better understanding of why her parents chose to stay together and that scared her even more.

Having an intelligent conversation with a baby about the latest big book or movie wasn't exactly possible. Since her friends were out or asleep when the baby went down for the night, she'd buried herself in being Mason's mom.

"Confession?" she asked.

He nodded, smiled at the reference to the game they used to play when they were about to reveal something they didn't want to or wanted to correct a lie.

"I work at a bar at night so I can spend the days with Mason. I don't feel like I've really slept in—well, if you count the pregnancy—almost two and a half years."

The look of shock on his face had her thinking sharing was a bad idea.

"I know I'm not using my degree," she said quickly, "but I will. As soon as Mason's old enough to go to school, I plan to get an office job. And then we'll have more of a normal life. I didn't want to miss it—miss this stage. I wanted to be there to see him take his first steps, hear him say his first words."

And, yes, to watch over him and make sure he wasn't showing any signs of the disease Bethany had died from. She'd never say that part out loud, but it was just as true.

"Of course, I'm also afraid that I'm doing everything wrong. Maybe I should get a normal job now with regular hours. I worry about being tired all the time. How can I possibly be a great mother on the days I can barely keep my eyes open?"

Dawson's silence was just about the worst thing right now as they got inside the car and then pulled out of the parking lot without him responding.

His mother's words echoed in Melanie's head over and over again until her brain hurt. *Leave my son alone. Let him have a life. Don't trap him with a child that would only make him live every day in fear.*

Well, guess what? The secret was out in the open. The ball was in Dawson's court. He knew he had a son. And now he was as trapped as her parents had been.

"You're a good mother," Dawson said, and the note of reverence in his voice took her back.

"How do you know?"

"The way you look at him. The way you want to protect him. Back on the porch you were ready to shoot me. *Me.*"

"In my defense, I didn't know who you were at the time," she said.

"Exactly my point. You didn't so much as flinch. You'd do whatever it took to keep him safe. You couldn't possibly be a bad mother. But we're not even close to done talking."

She held up a hand as she suppressed a yawn. Yeah, it was a stall tactic. What could she say to him?

Melanie remembered every moment of his sorrow after losing his sister.

Once the baby was born, her emotions had been on a perpetual roller coaster. Should she tell him? Did he have a right to know? Would it break him if the worst case came true? She'd been too exhausted and too emotional to make a rational decision, even though she told herself a thousand times she'd figure out a way to reach out to Dawson. Every time she seriously considered it, an image of him after he lost his sister, the overwhelming sadness had her reconsidering.

Coming back to Mason Ridge had been a colossal mistake. What if Dawson got it in his head that he needed to "do the right thing" and propose? She'd have to refuse. Visions of shared custody and an empty holiday table every other Christmas flooded her and tears instantly welled in her eyes. She was being silly, selfish. She knew that.

A few spilled over, but she'd be damned if she let Dawson see her cry. How many times had she heard her own mother crying herself to sleep at night?

Melanie had no plans to go there. Ever.

"WHERE ARE YOU taking us?" Melanie asked Dawson, his brain still trying to process everything that had just happened.

"Somewhere safe." A place where they could take care of the baby and talk. Dawson was owed answers. He would ask more questions, but he honestly didn't know where to start. Finding out he had a kid was more than a shock and he was trying to wrap his mind around how he felt about the news. Most men had nine months to gear up for parenthood. He'd had the bomb dropped in his lap about an hour ago. Not to mention the fact that he'd missed the first entire year and a half of his son's life.

Anger. Now, there was an emotion. Dawson was all too familiar with that reaction to the world. He'd be all over it now if he thought raging would do any good. It wouldn't. One thing Dawson had learned from youth was that no good had ever come out of losing his temper. He had more experience to back that statement than he wanted to admit.

Fear was another emotion ripping through him. What if his son had the same genetic trait Bethany had? What if Mason developed Alexander disease? A ripple of anger burned through Dawson.

Distrust topped his list, as well. People lied all the time. Dawson was ridiculous enough to believe that he and Melanie had a special relationship. If it had been, she wouldn't have been able to harbor a secret of that magnitude.

The pair had been inseparable as kids. She'd been the only one he could trust when his five-year-old sister had been diagnosed with a terminal illness. His parents had mentally checked out afterward. Not Melanie. She'd been there for him every step of the way.

Sadness and rage had filled the ten-year-old Dawson. He'd been angry at the world for taking away his baby, and she'd been called his baby from the day she was born for how protective of her he'd been.

There'd been endless doctor visits and the agony of watching his baby wither away until she'd closed her eyes for the last time.

Dawson had withdrawn from his friends that year and retreated inside himself into a dark place. Then, out of nowhere, Melanie had shown up. She'd just sat on his stairs every day after school until her parents called her in for supper, never once knocking. Days turned into weeks, weeks into months. Curiosity eventually got the best of Dawson and he opened the door and asked her what she wanted.

"Nothing," she'd said.

He'd closed the door and gone back into his room, stewing over why anyone would sit there every day on his property if she didn't have a good reason.

The next day they had the same conversation. After a week, he told her to leave.

She'd looked at him with the same eyes she had now, shivering, and gave him a flat "No."

When he asked why she wouldn't leave, she'd replied, "Free country."

That day, he'd sat down next to her. "You sure are stubborn."

"I know," was all she'd said. Then she'd pulled out a stack of basketball trading cards from her coat pocket— collecting had been his passion—and asked him what he'd give for a Topps Kareem Abdul-Jabbar 1976/1977 edition.

Dawson, who hadn't looked at his cards in almost a year, started negotiating for the forty dollar prize. As he did, the heavy burden he'd been carrying since losing his baby lost some of its grip. That had also been the first night he didn't cry himself to sleep.

It had taken a little time after that, but he'd eventually regained his bearings. He'd rejoined his friends, the rest of the world, and had shared everything with Melanie since then. He and Melanie had been inseparable until hormones and the demands of his high school girlfriend had split them apart.

Of all the people in the world, Dawson had believed that no matter how much time and space came between them, Melanie would always have his back.

Until now. Until this. Until her betrayal.

Never in his wildest thoughts would he have guessed she would do this to him—denying him his child burned him like a stray bolt of lightning, fast and deep. Hiding his son from him was the worst betrayal. She'd broken every thread of trust that had existed between them in a way that couldn't be repaired.

Dawson forced his thoughts back to the present as he exited the highway. He'd pulled a few evasive maneuvers to ensure that no one had followed them. There was a hotel on the outskirts of town, heading toward Dallas, that would work. They should be safe there for a little while at least.

Law enforcement knew about Sprigs and Alcorn, but Dawson couldn't rule out the possibility that there'd be others involved. Those two might sit at the top of the crime ring, but they had to have a fairly sophisticated network to pull off human trafficking. Any of their lackeys could be after Melanie.

Dawson had a thought. Maybe the guy back at the house was supposed to kidnap Melanie and bring her to Sprigs. With everyone on the lookout for him, he'd have to be crafty. He could've planned to snatch Melanie and then disappear out of the country.

The thought sat hot in Dawson's stomach. Being on the Most Wanted list made all those individuals even more dangerous. And that meant his son was in serious danger, too.

"Who knows about Mason?" he asked.

"My family."

"That's all?" he pressed. He'd picked up on something in her voice when she answered.

"Yes."

With a sick baby, Dawson's first priority would be to

get adequate housing and food. What did a baby eat? Did his son even eat real food? Dawson had no idea. Resentment for losing the past year and a half of his child's life bubbled to the surface along with a very real fear. Thinking about his little sister, her illness, had him wondering again if his son would inherit the disease.

He glanced at the rearview.

Melanie had closed her eyes in the backseat while holding Mason's hand, and a piece of Dawson's heart stirred.

Once again, he was floored at the thought he had a child.

It was a lot to digest, but nothing would stop him from getting there and accepting it. An image of him and Mason playing ball popped up in Dawson's head. Pride filled his chest, accompanied by a feeling he couldn't put his finger on. He recalled feeling something like this for his baby sister when she'd been alive, but the feeling had been tucked away so deep he almost forgot it had existed.

He hadn't allowed himself to think about her in years. He guessed he'd stashed away everything that had caused him pain.

His relationship with his parents had never been the same after her death. Their mourning was so powerful, so strong that they had nothing left to give Dawson or each other.

His mother took it the hardest, staying in bed until Dawson returned from school most days for a year. Griefstricken, she left her medical practice for almost two years before finally trying to move forward. His father put on a brave mask and went to work. He'd bring food home, keeping the house going, but he never really smiled or laughed after that.

A few years later one of Dawson's friends and her little brother, Rebecca and Shane, had been abducted. Dawson's parents had joined in the search. It was the first thing they'd done together since losing Bethany. With time, they became closer and more involved in Dawson's life again.

But in those dark years when the air had been sucked out of the house, Melanie had brought the light.

If someone had told him that Melanie would betray their history, their friendship, with one act, he wouldn't have believed it possible. She could've gotten away with almost anything and he'd have found a way to forgive her. But this?

Never.

Chapter Four

By the time Dawson pulled into the hotel parking lot, Melanie was asleep in the backseat. He hated to wake her, so he just stared at her for a minute. All those old feelings—good feelings, like nights spent outdoors looking up at the sky and warmth—crashed with the new reality, the one where she'd betrayed him in the worst way.

She wasn't the same person and neither was he. Her skin glowed and he figured something about motherhood had changed her. So much about her was different, especially in the way she carried herself. Her features had softened even more unless her son was threatened and then her protectiveness was written all over her stern gaze and determined stance.

On closer look, he'd noticed the dark circles under her eyes. It seemed she hadn't had a good night's sleep in months, and based on his limited experience with a baby, he could see how that might happen. Dawson didn't think he'd ever sleep again for worrying over his son, especially while the little guy was sick. Plus, everything about Mason seemed tiny and fragile.

The kid had a good set of lungs on him.

And Melanie seemed to think Mason was huge now. Dawson could only imagine what those first few months must've been like while he was even smaller.

"Where are we?" Melanie woke as soon as Dawson cut off the engine.

"We're in a Dallas suburb. Figured there'd be grocery stores nearby where we could pick up supplies for the baby."

She shook her head and blinked her eyes. "Okay. Just give me a second."

Dawson opened Mason's door and waited for her to unbuckle him. Working the car seat was a lesson for another day. He'd need to figure it out soon if he was going to take his son anywhere on his own. The learning curve on caring for a baby would be steep. He'd seen first-hand with his friend Dylan.

Melanie made it all look easy as she clicked a button and gently removed the straps to free their son.

Dawson reminded himself he'd only had two hours of practice, whereas she'd had the past eighteen months to adjust.

"You're tired. I'll carry the baby," Dawson said. No matter how bad things were between him and Melanie, Mason had nothing to do with it. Dawson had no plans to make his son feel uncomfortable when his parents were around each other so he'd have to work on keeping his emotions in check.

"No, thanks. I got him." Melanie scooped their son out of his seat fluidly. She had that same look in her eye that she did on the porch, too.

For now, Dawson wouldn't argue. But she'd learn to give him an inch. Mason belonged to both of them and Dawson had no plans to let his son down in the way his own parents had done him.

Grinding his back teeth, he shouldered the diaper bag.

After ten minutes at the front desk, Dawson had a hotel room key in hand and the promise that a crib was being delivered to the room. He knew enough to make sure there was a fridge and a microwave, opting for an all-suite hotel rather than one with traditional rooms. The inside entry would ensure that Melanie and Mason were safe while Dawson ran out for supplies.

Their suite was on the second floor, another safety precaution he'd insisted on.

"This should give us a place to rest and think so we can figure out our next move." He opened the door, allowing her and the baby in first.

"It might be safer for me and Mason if we go back to our apartment tomorrow. Sprigs doesn't know where I live."

He didn't want to scare her, but he couldn't let her take unnecessary risks with his child, either. "You're stuck with me until they catch him."

All hope that his comment would ease her concerns flew out the window with her exacerbated look. If possible, her stress levels seemed to increase. Hell on a stick. He hadn't meant for that to happen. She had bigger ghosts from her past to be afraid of than him.

Mason stirred, spit out his pacifier and started crying again.

The sound was pitiful and caused Dawson's heart to sink to his toes. He'd do just about anything to make it go away. Watching his son upset with no means to soothe him had never made Dawson feel more helpless in his life, not since…well…dammit…he couldn't go there again about his sister.

Melanie was gently bouncing Mason while she sang the song from the car to him.

The place had everything they needed, including a bedroom with a door that closed, sealing off the room. He figured Melanie would appreciate that feature as much as he did about now. Especially if they had to stay put for a few days.

"Is he hungry? Does he need milk or formula?" Dawson had scooped up the pacifier and set it on the counter.

"No, he shouldn't be. Babies cry when they don't feel good." She kissed Mason's forehead. "He's just telling us that whatever he has isn't fun."

Dawson stripped off his shirt and paced. He oversaw the logistics department for a major online retailer. He could handle this. He thought about his friend Dylan. There was a man who was the second least likely natural father material in their group and look how well he'd done since his daughter, Maribel, had come to live with him. To say the guy had changed drastically was a lot like saying a cow had turned into a dog.

Dawson mentally calculated the age difference between Maribel and Mason. She was three, so the two were about a year and a half apart. Thinking back, she'd come to live with her father when she was about six months older than Mason.

At least Dawson had a friend with experience at being thrown this curve ball. Dylan would be a great resource. Dawson needed to reach out to his friend when things settled down and he was able to spend time alone with his son. As protective as Melanie was, there was no risk she'd leave the two of them to their own resources before she had to.

As much as he didn't like the idea of being forced to spend time with her after what she'd done, he wasn't stupid. He would need her to help him get up to speed. Baby boys probably weren't much different from girls, but Dawson was starting from ground zero with the whole parenting thing, and he needed all the help he could get.

A few minutes of rocking and singing later, and Mason had settled down enough to go back to sleep.

"What time is it?" Melanie asked, diverting her gaze from him as a soft knock came at the door.

If that noise woke the baby, the person on the other side of that hunk of wood had better run. A glance at Mason revealed that he still slept.

Dawson checked through the peephole and saw two men dressed in maintenance jumpsuits standing on the other side. No doubt the crib had arrived.

He opened the door slightly and put his finger to his lips.

One of the men, the one nearest the door, nodded his understanding and then turned to his buddy and repeated the gesture.

Dawson allowed them access.

"Where would you like this set up?" the lead man whispered.

Dawson deferred to Melanie. An act he was sure to repeat more than he cared to in the coming days, weeks, months.

And yet she looked just as sweet and pitiful as Mason with the boy snuggled against her chest. Dawson didn't want to notice either of those things any more than he wanted to feel sorry for her. He did.

HAVING DAWSON AROUND fried Melanie's nerves. Thank the stars he'd gone out for milk and baby food after he washed up and rinsed blood from his shirt. At least now she could breathe normally again—something that was impossible to do when he was in the room.

The maintenance workers had put together the crib. Thankfully, Dawson had stuck around until they'd left, and he was all she could think about since he walked out the door.

She'd given Mason a second dose of medicine according to the directions on the package.

He'd made a good point earlier, though. Why was Sprigs still obsessed with her? There had to be some underlying reason. If she could figure it out maybe she could make it stop. She understood why their other friends had been targeted. They'd been sitting on secrets that, pieced together, could've gotten Beckett Alcorn and Sprigs arrested a lot sooner and broken up the child abduction scheme.

But what had Melanie done?

Nothing.

She'd been careful not to encourage Sprigs. Then again, it wasn't as if she'd remember something that had happened fifteen years ago. Good God, she could barely remember events from last week. Lack of sleep didn't do good things to the memory. Or the brain. Or the body, she mused, looking down at her little pooch. Her stomach muscles hadn't quite bounced back since she had the baby, and most of the time she didn't care. It wasn't as if she was trying to date.

Being in the room with Dawson had made her think about just how much she'd let herself go. Her hair was in a perpetual ponytail and she lived in yoga pants. She had to get dressed up for work, but that didn't count. Forget makeup unless it was time to clock in.

Then she'd force herself into a pair of jeans, put on an actual bra and rotate her three good shirts. Money had been tight and all of hers had gone to taking care of Mason. Another thing she didn't regret.

But speaking of clothes, she'd left her parents' house in such a rush she hadn't had a chance to grab any. Which was fine for now. At least she'd thrown on yoga pants when she heard the noise outside. Other than that, she had on a sleeping T-shirt and no bra.

And thinking about that was just a way of distracting herself from the very real possibility that Dawson would take her son away.

A part of her knew that he could never be that cruel, but if the shoe were on the other foot, what would she think about him?

She pushed the thought aside because she'd been trying to protect him.

Plus, there was no time to worry about that while she was hiding out from a crazy person—a man who stole kids.

A shudder ran through her bone-tired body. She'd been focused on the possibility of Dawson filing for sole custody, but there was another very real threat out there to her son. The Mason Ridge Abductor was more than one person, and the second half of that team seemed intent on harming her.

The door opened, causing her to jump.

"It's me," Dawson said, arms full of bags. "I got whole milk. That's what he drinks, right?"

"Yeah, sorry, I should've been specific."

"It's fine. I looked it up on my cell. Apparently, you can learn just about everything on the internet."

She couldn't help herself so she laughed at his attempt at humor. She shouldn't like the way it made him smile. At this point, she had no idea what his plans were and she had to protect her son at all costs. The thought of not being with him would end her—Mason was the only thing she'd thought about for two and a half years.

"I'll help you put away the groceries," she offered.

"Sit down. I got this." He waved her off.

She bit back a yawn. When was the last time she'd really slept? Certainly not at her parents' place. The idea had been good. Come back to Mason Ridge to help her friend while Abby took care of Mason in Houston. It was the first time she'd been away from him and she'd totally underestimated how much her heart would ache without him there.

A couple nights of sleep would help her be a better mother, she'd reasoned. Had any of that worked out the way she'd planned?

Only if tipping off his father to his existence was part of the plan.

Being away from her baby had only caused her to worry more about Mason, miss him and try to ignore the fact that his father, the man she'd never stopped loving, was sleeping right across the street. She'd known he was visiting because of his black SUV and a part of her had wished he'd been there because of his feelings for her even though she'd feared running into him, afraid of his questions. If he'd seen her face-to-face, would he realize something was different about her? Would he figure it out? Would he care?

Okay, so that last part had been answered with a resounding yes. But it wasn't an emotion reserved for her, it was for Mason. There'd never been a doubt in her mind that if Dawson had known about Mason he would want to do the right thing and be involved. Because he was truly a good guy, he would most likely even propose marriage. In her hormonal state, she might've agreed. And then what? If Mason did have the gene, God forbid, and ended up with the same fate as Bethany, Dawson would be stuck with Melanie forever. The only tie they'd had, Mason, would be gone. And their lives would be empty.

At least her parents had had two daughters as glue for their relationship.

Considering the other side of the coin, say Mason escaped the worst-case scenario. This was the one she prayed for every night. If she and Dawson had married based on her pregnancy, would all the spark between them slowly die with the realization that the only reason they were together was Mason?

Most nights, Melanie sat up worrying, churning over her guilt. She stressed about Mason growing up never knowing his father, about Dawson's reaction if he found out about his son, and about whether or not she was being unfair. And it had just felt like this huge no-win situation. Tell Dawson and commit him to a life of worry. Don't tell him and cheat him out of his son.

How many nights had she lain awake staring at the ceiling? That hamster wheel of questions spinning through her mind? Wishing answers would magically appear?

Working nights mostly after he was asleep, she felt incredibly blessed to have been there for all his important firsts. There would be even more that she had to look forward to, like his first day of kindergarten, his first bike ride and the first book he could read on his own. Based on his taste so far it would be something by Dr. Seuss.

"That about does it," Dawson said. She hadn't noticed the little clanking noises had stopped that he'd made while putting away supplies.

Another yawn rolled up and out before she could suppress it. When was the last time she'd been this tired? Having her body beyond the brink of exhaustion was one thing. Her mind, overthinking her circumstance, had pushed this into a whole new stratosphere.

"Think you can get some sleep?" he asked.

"I doubt it."

"I've never seen you look so tired."

"Comes with the job," she mused, thankful the mood had lightened at least for now. "Thanks for what you said earlier, by the way."

His brow came up as he took a seat on the couch. "And that was?"

"For saying I was a good mother."

"Whatever is going on between us, and believe me, we're going to talk about this all very soon, doesn't affect how I think of you as Mason's mother." He paused thoughtfully. "I meant every word of what I said. He couldn't have done better."

The deep rumble of his voice, the way it poured over her like Amaretto on vanilla ice cream, would cause her knees to buckle if she'd been standing. He'd always had that ability to make her legs turn into rubber.

"It means a lot to hear you say that, Dawson."

"Come sit over here on the couch," he said, motioning for her to take a seat next to him.

She did, feeling the heat swirl as their shoulders touched. He still had that effect on her and she should be concerned about that. As it was, she was just happy that she could feel that way for anyone. To say her love life had been a draught since getting pregnant was the understatement of the year.

Walking away from Dawson had been one of the most difficult things she'd ever done. Until sitting next to him on the couch right now.

Chapter Five

Dawson urged Melanie to put her head on his shoulder as he leaned deeper into the sofa, tabling his anger for now.

If they were going to coparent, they were going to have to learn to work together. None of that could happen in her current condition and his former state of mind. She was run-down, skittish and exhausted, and he couldn't help feeling partly to blame. As it was, he'd been throwing a lot of subtle anger at her. Not that he wasn't still mad.

Right now he acknowledged that it was more important to set his own frustration aside and do what was right for Mason. And that involved making sure his mother took better care of herself.

As soon as he figured out what to do about Sprigs so they could set this ordeal behind them, Dawson would take the necessary steps to ensure that Mason had everything he needed. First order of business would be figuring out an appropriate amount of child support. Melanie was stubborn. She'd argue about taking the money. He could see that it was important for her to feel as though she was taking care of her son.

Dawson could tighten his own belt enough to swing paying her bills.

A noise shot straight through him. He held steady, and

that was a good thing, because that small, honking-like-a-duck sound came out of Melanie.

She was asleep on his shoulder and that shouldn't give him satisfaction.

It did.

MELANIE WOKE WITH a start and quickly scanned the room. Dawson was pacing in front of the window, holding Mason. The image of him shirtless, with their son against his chest, could melt a glacier in Antarctica. She wouldn't be able to erase that picture for a long time, and maybe a little piece of her heart didn't want to. "How is he?"

"His fever is down and he hasn't coughed again."

"That's great news." Maybe life could be like this? Dawson could pitch in to help share some of the load. His mother was wrong. He looked pretty happy holding his son. "I should change his diaper."

"Changed it when he woke up. That wasn't as easy as it looks. On the internet they use a baby doll to demonstrate. This little guy doesn't hold still." Dawson seemed pleased with himself.

Melanie had worked so hard at creating a life for herself and Mason without really including others. She'd moved to Houston to get away from Dawson, but that had also separated her from her family and any help they could give. Her sister was busy with college in Austin. Maybe it was time to let someone else in. "Did you get any sleep?"

"No."

"I can take Mason for a while. Let you get some shuteye." She made a move to get up.

Dawson waved her off.

"Not necessary. I don't need that much rest. Plus, I

was doing some thinking. We should talk." He paused—
so not a good sign—and she prepared for the bombshell
he was about to drop.

"Mind if I get a cup of coffee first?" she asked, needing to put off the conversation until she had enough caffeine inside her to handle what was sure to come next. A
discussion about Dawson in their life, permanently.

"You don't drink coffee," he said.

"I need caffeine and I'd kill for a toothbrush right now."

"You'll find that and toothpaste in the bathroom.
Pepsi's in the fridge. I had the store manager cut up some
limes and there's ice in the bucket." He motioned toward
the counter. Sure enough, ice and a glass waited.

"Seriously?" Okay, now she knew she was dreaming.

A few minutes later, clean teeth sealed the deal. This
felt too good to be real life.

"That's still how you like it, right?" he asked as she
walked into the room.

"Yeah. I just didn't think—"

"What? I'd remember?"

"That you'd care." She pulled out the baggy of wedge-
sliced limes from the pint-size fridge.

"If you doubted my feelings before, then you don't
need to anymore. I'm 'all in' with everything connected
to this little boy." His tone was laced with just enough ice
to send a chill rippling down her back. It wasn't much,
not enough for someone who didn't know him to pick up
on, but she knew.

He bounced the baby on his knee and Mason was too
happy for her to ruin the moment by shooting a zinger
back. Besides, she didn't want to start a fight in front of
him, and since she was about to have her favorite drink
courtesy of Dawson, she decided to let his comments slide
as she fixed her soda.

Ice in a glass, followed by Pepsi and then the lime and this was shaping up to be the best morning she'd had in a long while. She took a sip and could've sworn she heard angels sing. "I slept crazy-good on that couch last night." She glanced at the clock. "Correction, this morning. Thanks for seeing to Mason."

"He needed his breakfast and you have to take better care of yourself."

So much for polite conversation.

Melanie decided nothing would ruin her first Pepsi. She walked over to the small table and chairs nestled in the corner rather than sit in the living area.

Not having to rush around to change Mason's diaper and fix him something to eat left her feeling a little useless. This should be a glorious time. Had she forgotten how to have an easy morning? This wasn't exactly a normal situation. She tried her best to ignore the big presence on the chair, but he seemed intent on sweating her out.

"Okay. Fine. What did you want to discuss?" she asked.

Dawson was on his feet. He made a beeline toward her, and her pulse beat faster with every step he came closer. She set her Pepsi down in time to receive Mason.

"Do you smell that?" he asked, turning his attention toward the appliances.

"No. What?" She sniffed near Mason's diaper, grateful that wasn't the kind of scent he was talking about.

"Did you leave anything on in the bathroom?"

"Like what? There's only a hair dryer in there. I think you'd hear it." She glanced around the room, and must've seen the smoke at the same time as he did.

Dawson raced toward the door to the hallway and placed his hand on it. "It's hot. We're not going out that way."

"That's not good." Melanie tamped down the panic rising in her chest.

"No. It isn't."

"Why aren't the smoke detectors going off?" She motioned toward the sprinkler on the ceiling.

"Good question. The control panel might've been disabled," he said with a frustrated grunt.

"This can't be related to us, can it? How would anyone know we were here?" she asked.

"I thought we'd be safe all the way out here. Whoever set the fire might've located your car in the parking lot." Dawson disappeared into the bathroom and she heard water running. Melanie found a phone and called 9-1-1.

It took two minutes in total to report the fire.

Dawson returned a few seconds later and placed the towels at the base of the door, sealing off the room. "We're not getting out that way, so that means we have to use our other option."

Melanie glanced around the room as Dawson disappeared into the bedroom. She had no idea what options he was talking about.

"I'm going to close this door so I don't scare the baby when I break the window," he said as he appeared in the doorway.

"Okay. I'll gather up supplies." She let Mason stand by himself at the coffee table. He was a good walker but could get ahead of himself and end up on his back side.

Melanie spent the next five minutes packing the diaper bag.

A crash sounded as the sirens blared in the distance.

Dawson appeared in the room a moment later. "We can't leave until the firemen get here. There's no way to get him down safely. This whole scenario makes me think someone's trying to flush us out."

"I hear the sirens." Smoke was creeping in through the vents causing Melanie to cough.

Dawson picked up Mason and held him tight to his chest. "Let's bring him in the other room where the air is clear."

The little boy angled his body toward the floor, started wiggling and winding up to cry.

"He wants down. What should I do?" The big strong Dawson looked at a loss for the first time since this ordeal had started last night.

Melanie held out her hands, trying to see if her son would come to her. Mason let out a whimper and shook his head.

"Come on, baby."

His answer was still no.

She located her keys in the diaper bag and jingled them. He took the bait this time and angled his body toward her.

Dawson jumped into action the second they hit the next room. He wet towels and stuffed them under the door to prevent smoke from filling the bedroom. And then he paced.

The next ten minutes waiting for the firemen to arrive were excruciating.

Dawson was signaling the firefighters in the lot as they roared up to the building.

Once they were discovered, it didn't take but a few more seconds for a safety ladder to be placed against the wall and a fireman to climb the rungs.

Melanie handed over her baby and then followed the fireman down. Dawson was already there by the time she set foot on the ground. He'd wasted no time jumping out the window and had managed to bring the diaper bag with him.

Since it was midday, there were fewer cars in the parking lot. About twenty people stood around, watching the building to see what would happen next. A few others milled around.

With the noise and commotion, it would be easy for Sprigs to hide among the onlookers, so she held Mason tighter to her chest.

Dawson kept her tucked behind him, scanning the lot as he waited their turn to give statements.

"We'll need to stick around a little while. Stay close," Dawson said, his gaze scanning the lot, keeping his body between her and everyone else. He motioned toward an officer and whispered to her, "This place isn't safe and I don't want either of you out of my sight."

Chapter Six

Melanie strapped Mason securely in his car seat. It hadn't taken long to give her statement to the officer a few minutes ago, since it was the same as Dawson's. They'd also relayed their belief that this could be connected to the case in Mason Ridge. The officer had taken notes and then promised to connect to the sheriff's office.

"It might be best to get out of Texas for a few days until this whole thing blows over," Dawson said.

"I have to work tonight and I need this job."

"I'm not sure I like the idea of you going back to work until we sort this out." He moved to the driver's side, so she handed him the keys.

She didn't want to remind him of the fact that she'd had a life before last night that she needed to get back to, a safe life that didn't include home invasions and arson.

"Do you think he's here?" She glanced around. An uneasy feeling settled in her stomach.

"Might be. Either way, we're not taking the chance."

Dawson snaked out of the parking lot and then hopped on and off the highway a couple of times, checking the rearview.

"Sprigs had to be involved with that fire, didn't he? It's too coincidental," she said.

"Do you remember when the Sno-Kone building burned down?" Dawson asked.

"Yeah, I do. It was during one of the hottest summers, late July. They never caught the guy."

"Dylan saw Sprigs watching from in between cars in the parking lot. He set the fire." Dawson changed lanes.

"I remember specifically that they never caught the guy. Why didn't Dylan go to the cops?"

He slanted a look at her and then returned his full attention to the stretch of highway in front of them.

"Right. With Dylan's criminal history they wouldn't have believed him," she said, deflated.

"Or worse, they would've accused him of doing it instead."

"Why would anyone report a crime they committed themselves?" The sheriff's department needed a serious overhaul. She doubted Sheriff Brine would hold office much longer given his personal association with the Alcorns. The senior Alcorn might've been cleared of suspicion, although he had to have been covering, but his son was guilty. And he was going to do the prison time.

"People do crazy things and Dylan isn't stupid," Dawson said. "Which is why he didn't get caught for most of the stuff he pulled."

"I can't believe how much he's changed."

Dawson quirked a glance at her.

"I've been in touch with a couple of the girls. They've been keeping me up-to-date," she clarified.

"He straightened himself out in the military." Dawson changed lanes again. "I'm guessing the attack on your parents' house was a crime of opportunity and that means Sprigs or one of his people is watching you. The guy from last night most likely works for Sprigs. When he didn't get the job done, Sprigs may have decided to step up and take care of it himself at the hotel."

"Except these are just theories. We have no evidence and we can't prove anything," she said.

"True. Rest assured that I have every intention of ensuring your safety personally." His tone left no room for doubt.

"No one knows where I live in Houston. I've kept my address private from everyone but my family, Lisa and Samantha. Those are the only people who can track me down," she said.

"You're going to have to open your circle a little wider, you know, now that everything's changed."

She didn't respond. He was talking about himself and, most likely, his family.

"And I've been thinking about something else, too. I don't want you to work. Not while Mason's little and you have to sling drinks at some bar," he said, matter-of-factly.

"Not a chance. I don't want to depend on anyone else for a check."

"We haven't been off to a good start here and I'll take responsibility for my part. However, I get a say in how my son's brought up from here on out, and I don't want his mother working in a bar. Period."

Period? Did Dawson suddenly get to dictate her life? How would that work out for her? The idea of being home with Mason and not being exhausted all the time was serious nirvana to her, but not like this. Not when she'd have to watch the mailbox every month for a check from Dawson, or set her phone on alert to be notified if he made a deposit in her bank account. Just the thought of being completely dependent on someone else made a hot rash creep up her chest. She'd worked too hard for her independence.

"No can do. End of story," she said a little too emphatically.

"I beg to differ."

"You don't get to step in and tell me how to run my life, Dawson."

"I'm offering you an opportunity here. I thought you'd want to grab on to it. Why does it frustrate you? You said you wanted to spend more time with Mason." That he sounded genuinely confused didn't help matters.

"I do."

"Then why are you being so stubborn?"

Is that what he thought? He didn't have hordes of money stashed in a bank account somewhere. He worked for a living, and he'd started saving for his own ranch when he was a kid. No way would she take his savings away from him. *He'd resent it if I did*, a little voice in the back of her mind said. Owning his own ranch had been his dream since he was a little boy. And he'd been waking up early and driving into Dallas for a job at a major online retailer running logistics that he didn't like for a very long time to make it come true. Even though his parents had more than enough money to fund any venture Dawson set his sights on, he was too proud to take their handout. Precisely the reason he should understand her position.

"It's important for me to take care of us, and I've been doing a pretty darn good job of it so far," she said.

"Just like that?" came out half hurt, half growl.

It was better for her to upset him now than to be the reason he had to abandon his future.

"Thank you, though. I do appreciate the thought. It's just that I need to be able to take care of things on my own."

"Like you have been by shutting me out?" he countered.

"I'm sorry about my decision up to this point when it comes to you and Mason. But my life is a different story. I make the calls. You'll be involved with your son. I get that. And we'll work out a decent schedule for visitation later."

"Visitation?"

"Oh, I assumed you wanted to be part of Mason's life. I totally understand if that's not the case." Was she off base?

"Try and keep me away." His low timbre sent a different kind of shiver down her neck.

Was that a threat? She decided to let it slide. They were both stressed and that had their nerves on edge. Dawson wouldn't stay mad at her for long. And she had his best interest at heart. He'd see that eventually.

In the meantime, this was going to be one long car trip. One hour down, four to go. *Oh joy!*

Mason had nodded off in the backseat, which meant that Ms. Waverly, the babysitter, was going to have an interesting time watching him tonight. Or, more likely, Melanie was going to have a tough time tomorrow considering he didn't do so well when his schedule was off track. Toddlers craved routine.

But then, what if Sprigs figured out where she lived? Would he come for her? Mason could get hurt in the cross fire. Anxiety engulfed her like a wildfire.

"I've done everything I can to keep my information private, but what if he finds me in Houston?" She couldn't keep panic from her voice.

"He won't. And if he does, I'll be there to stop him."

"You can't stay at my place forever. You have work to get back to. Your life is in Mason Ridge."

"Let me worry about that," he said. "Besides, every law enforcement agency is looking for him right now. You're on high alert and he's been getting away with his crimes for a long time because he's not stupid."

"He could hurt Mason to get back at me." Her voice sounded small even to her. "Maybe I should call my parents and ask them to pick him up. He could go on the road with them for a little while."

The idea of being separated from her son even for a short period knifed her heart, but she clamped down the pain. There was no way she'd risk her son's safety just so she could see him every day.

"Let's look at this logically. You could call your folks and have them take him on the road. If Sprigs is determined to get to you, then he could track them down. They're older, unsuspecting—"

"I'd tell them what was going on, Dawson."

"Fine. Even if they know what they're getting into, that doesn't mean they can keep him safer than we can, than *I* can. I don't like the idea of being apart. Not when our son could be used against you."

"You have a good argument," she conceded. She'd be relieved if not for the fear settling over her. No matter how much this felt like a bad dream, this was real and it might not be going away any time soon.

"No one's taking our son." Dawson's words, the determination in them, brought a wave of comfort over her fried nerves.

"You're right," she said. "I'm not going back to Mason Ridge and neither is Mason."

"For now, I'll agree to those terms. I'll tell my family about my son as soon as we get better acquainted and then they'll want to be part of his life, too."

It shouldn't wrench Melanie's stomach that Mason would have so many more people in his life to love him. She couldn't think of that without the selfish thought that meant she'd get so much less of him. No matter how she looked at it, there was no way she could or would deny his father or grandparents visitation.

However, the conversation with his mother might not go as smoothly as Dawson assumed. He didn't have any idea what the woman had said to a newly pregnant Melanie that made her hightail it out of town.

Heck, Melanie had been so naive that for half of her pregnancy she'd expected Dawson to show up, thinking that surely his mother would've shared the news at some point. She hadn't, so Melanie had kept up her end of the bargain. The way she'd read his mother's threat was that she got to keep her son if she disappeared.

Over time, Melanie had let go of the fear his mother would follow through. The woman had only wanted Melanie to disappear.

Dawson would still be in the dark about his son if Melanie hadn't gone to Mason Ridge. Even though she was terrified of the future and of the coming changes, she couldn't regret that decision now.

Dawson knew.

All her cards were on the table for everyone to see, or soon would be. Didn't that leave a sinking feeling in the pit of her stomach? Having Dawson around played havoc with her mentally and physically. And she was already exhausted from both. The thought of bringing more people into the equation didn't exactly calm her stress levels.

The rest of the drive was unsettling save for the fact that Mason slept most of the way. He'd barely coughed and she figured the reason he was sleeping so much was that his body was fighting the virus.

Getting home to her own apartment was the best part of her day.

The strong possibility that Sprigs was still near Mason Ridge made her even happier to be in Houston. In fact, she didn't care what Dawson said, she had no plans to return to her hometown after all that had happened. Not until Sprigs was safely locked behind bars. Maybe not even then.

She didn't care what Dawson thought about her plans, either. He could come to Houston for a visit to his son anytime he wanted to.

Even though it was inevitable, she didn't want to negotiate with Dawson. She still remembered how broken he'd been when he lost his sister, because it was the same look that was on his face when he realized her son was his child, too.

Was his mother right? Would Dawson always hold her in contempt for bringing back those old hurts?

Was it somehow making it all worse that he found out about Mason this way? Heck if Melanie knew what the best path was anymore.

No relationship, no matter how strong or steeped in history, could survive that betrayal. She'd known that on some level when she made the deal with the devil in the first place. She'd been scared, hormonal and alone, and his mother had pounced on the opportunity to put Melanie in her place—a place below the Hill family. In Alice Hill's opinion, Melanie had never been good enough for Dawson.

Seeing the hurt in his eyes—hurt she'd put there—Melanie couldn't argue with the woman's point.

MELANIE'S APARTMENT MIGHT lack in square footage but it made up for it in charm. The place was all her, and Dawson didn't want to instantly feel at home there even though he did.

The living area was open to the kitchen with a large pass-through in between. She'd placed a couple of beige bar stools there. A couch and a pair of chairs flanked the fireplace. The wood mantel had several candid pictures of her and Mason. Dawson could see the age progression in the photos and part of him wondered who'd taken the shots. Jealousy roared through him at the thought of another man being around his son. *And Melanie. Touching Melanie.*

Okay, fine. He didn't like the idea of another man's hands on Melanie, but she wasn't exactly territory he had the right to claim no matter how possessive he felt. Seeing his son in her arms didn't help with that particular emotion and Dawson figured he needed to get used to all this. She wasn't going away. He wasn't going away. And there could be a man in her life…no… Dawson couldn't even go there in thought.

No other man got to spend more time with his son than him. *Or with Melanie,* a little voice inside his head said. Dawson would like to quash that cursed little voice, too. He didn't need to have feelings for her, especially since he was already jealous thinking of a make-believe guy spending time with her and Mason.

Dawson needed to sort out his crazy emotions and come up with a plan for making this arrangement work. If not for his logistics job in Dallas, he'd consider relocating to Houston to be closer to his son. Then again, he could always find another job once the dust settled.

How would Melanie react? That's where the confusion began. It wasn't the fact that he'd had a son with Melanie that threw Dawson. It was that she didn't trust him no matter how well he knew him—and Melanie knew him better than anyone else. Then there was the simple fact that she was the one who'd kept his child from him and *she* looked at him suspiciously anyway.

Forget that he'd been naive enough to think they'd had

a strong bond as kids. A spark had ignited when they'd started a *fling*, wasn't that what she'd called it before she left?

He'd been confused, hurt when she'd pushed him away before, and it made even less sense now. He was, after all, the father of their child and trying to help.

"Would you mind changing Mason's diaper while I get his dinner ready?" she asked.

"Got it." Dawson started toward the little tyke. He ran down the hall, squealing in delight. What a different picture from last night.

After completing the task, he returned. He leaned his hip against the kitchen counter, essentially blocking her in. "How about I watch Mason tonight while you work?"

"You're not serious. And I need to feed him so I can get ready."

"Oh, but I am. Give Ms. Whoever the night off. I'm here. I'll just be fumbling around waiting for you otherwise."

"Are you kidding me? You barely learned how to change a diaper today. It's too much, too soon."

There she was, not trusting him again and it hurt more than he cared to acknowledge. "I can take care of my own son."

"All I'm saying is give it more time."

"You'll save money this way. You'll be at work with a lot of people around you. Sprigs doesn't know where you live, but we can't be too cautious, not after what happened at the hotel." Even she couldn't argue his logic there. "How old is the babysitter?"

"She's old. And you have a point. I don't want to put her at risk unnecessarily."

Capitalizing on his good fortune, he added, "You can write down his evening routine. I'll follow it to the letter."

She stood there for a long moment, contemplating, tapping her toe on the tile. She had that look on her face, the one that said he was wearing her down. Time to be quiet and let her decide. The longer she took to make up her mind, the better for him. At least some things hadn't changed about her.

"Okay. You win." She jotted down a list with a satisfied little smirk, which he didn't quite understand. "It's easier to bathe Mason in the sink than in the tub."

"Got it." He took the list.

"Are you sure?"

"I said I was good to go," he said.

"Okay. You have my number. Call if you have any questions. Anything comes up and I can be home in twenty minutes if needed."

"We'll be fine. Besides, I have this—" he held up his cell "—if I need you."

"That reminds me. I haven't charged my phone for the past twenty-four hours. No way do I have battery left," she said.

"Where's the charger? I'll plug it in while you get ready for work."

"Thanks. That's really helpful." She looked surprised.

"We can get along when we try, Melanie." He regretted the words as soon as they left his mouth. They'd made progress in the past fifteen minutes toward him not being so angry and her actually giving him real responsibility with Mason. Dawson was going to need to figure out how to put the past behind him if he was going to give his son the life he deserved. And Mason deserved for his parents to work together on his behalf. "I'm sorry I said that."

"It's fine." Her chin came up defiantly. "You're right. We're both adults."

"I'm working on it." He tried to make a joke to lighten the mood.

"I hope we can make peace for Mason's sake," she said before disappearing to get ready for work.

That was exactly what he intended to do. He made himself comfortable on the floor, playing cars with Mason.

When Melanie stepped in the room after getting dressed, Dawson also regretted staying home to watch the baby rather than sit at the bar and watch over her.

The jeans she wore fit her like a second set of skin and she had the curves to prove it. Her white blouse over a black bra showed just enough lace to get Dawson's imagination going. Her breasts, though covered, were fuller than he remembered. She had more curves, and his body betrayed him by instantly reacting to her beauty.

With her shiny hair long and loose around her shoulders, he almost decided it was a good time to revisit his earlier argument about her not working at all.

"Ma-ma." Mason bolted across the room toward her.

The blouse she was wearing was buttoned up and Dawson figured that was for his and Mason's benefit. Imagining her shirt opened a little more wasn't a good idea.

"You look fantastic, Melanie," he said, and his voice was deeper than he'd intended.

Chapter Seven

The baby started crying before Melanie got out the door. Dawson wondered how a kid could go from smiling, happy-go-lucky, playing on the floor to full-on tears and tantrum so quickly and suddenly, as if someone had flipped a switch.

Worse yet, Melanie calmed the child long enough to leave. And then the second wave hit.

Loud. Heartbreaking. Helpless.

"It's okay, little guy." Dawson tried to soothe him, unsure if picking the toddler up would make things worse.

The little boy's fist went into his mouth and then he choked on slobber.

How on earth had Melanie figured all this out on her own?

The boy couldn't be hungry. He'd eaten half an hour ago.

All Dawson was supposed to have to do was to give the kid a bath and then put him to bed. It wasn't supposed to be this hard, or gut wrenching. Hearing the little guy cry was ripping Dawson's heart out of his chest. His stress level was through the roof.

His pride wouldn't let him call Melanie for help.

There had to be something he could do to calm him.

Dawson scanned the room for something, anything

that might distract the child. TV. That should work. He located the remote on the coffee table and clicked on the TV.

The cartoon added to the noise factor. Dawson held his arms out toward the boy to see if he wanted to be held.

That elicited a scream so loud the neighbor tapped on the adjacent wall. Dawson didn't want to get Melanie in trouble with her apartment complex. What had she used earlier to calm Mason? Keys. Dawson searched for a set. No, Melanie had taken hers with her. He'd left his parents' place in such a rush to check on her last night that he'd forgotten his own, which reminded him that he needed to call his parents and let them know he wouldn't be back for a while.

No keys.

There wasn't much else Dawson could do, so he brought his son juice. Dawson was so flustered that he stubbed his toe on the leg of the coffee table, bit back a word he couldn't say in front of his son, and then hopped around on his good foot. What he wouldn't give for a strong drink right about then.

Mason laughed.

Dawson thought he might not have heard correctly. So he pretended to hurt his toe this time and was rewarded with a full belly laugh.

"Oh, you like that?"

A pair of red-rimmed eyes stared up at him. So he did the only thing he could…picked up a toy and smacked himself upside the head with it.

Mason roared with laughter.

Making his son happy made something else happen inside Dawson…something he couldn't put his finger on. It was fragile but not fleeting.

Rather than analyze what any of that meant, Dawson asked, "Ready for a bath?"

The little boy's face lit up as he sniffled and then coughed. Crying must've aggravated his chest.

Dawson had never felt so on edge. One wrong move and a torrent of those crocodile tears would be rolling down Mason's cheeks again. Dawson had never felt so vulnerable in his life.

He scooped his son off the floor and into his arms.

There was a resource he'd be tapping into later, his friend Dylan. But Dawson didn't want to share this news with anyone just yet. Not until he wrapped his own mind around it.

Mason started winding up to cry again.

Was there something else Melanie had given him to quiet him? Oh. Right. A pacifier. Dawson dashed over to the diaper bag and located a clean one.

The little boy was satisfied the second he popped it in his mouth.

And that made Dawson very happy.

Melanie had told Dawson it was easier to bathe Mason in the sink.

There were toys in the bath. Mason wiggled in Dawson's arms, indicating he wanted to get down.

Dawson obliged, careful not to set off another round of crying and, therefore, coughing.

He managed to get his son through a bath in the tub with minimal tears, but Dawson was on edge the entire time. Getting on Mason's pajamas was another issue. The little squirt refused.

Trying again, Dawson was pleased with himself when he managed to dress his son only to find his clothes littering the hallway. By the third attempt, Dawson was happy to get a T-shirt on his child.

What was wrong with sleeping in a T-shirt and a diaper? Putting the kid to bed should be easy, right?

No. That brought on a whole new wave of tears and cries for his mama.

Refusing to admit defeat, Dawson popped a cartoon into the DVD player. Given that there were twenty different DVDs with the same animal on the cover, Dawson figured this was his son's favorite show.

He settled onto the couch with Mason curled up on his chest.

MELANIE EASED HER key into the lock, slowly opened the door and tiptoed across the threshold. It was quarter to three in the morning on a pitch-black night.

Inside, light from the TV filled the space. She stopped midstride when she got a good look at what was on her couch. Her heart squeezed at the sight of Mason curled up on his father's chest, both sleeping.

They looked so natural together. She'd expected at least one frantic phone call while she was at work. Dawson seemed to have handled everything like a pro. And that was every reason she should keep her guard up.

The thought occurred to her that he could have a great case to reverse custody. The courts might just decide in his favor. She would be the one with visitation rather than the other way around. Panic filled her, causing her to shake. She couldn't lose Mason. He'd become her world and that was exactly how she wanted it.

There was another thing Melanie had forced out of her thoughts far too often. The disease that had claimed Dawson's sister so young. Bethany was five when the devastating diagnosis came. Over a short period, Dawson had watched his baby sister lose her ability to walk, talk and smile. He'd said not being able to make her laugh anymore was the worst part. Melanie figured he didn't want to remember those horrible final months until his sister had gone peacefully in her sleep.

She'd seen firsthand how difficult his sister's death had been on his family. Having a child of her own gave her a deeper understanding of just how hard, how unfair, that had been. His mother, a physician, who couldn't heal her own daughter. No wonder the woman had become so bitter.

Melanie didn't think she'd be the same way, but then she hadn't walked in that woman's shoes, either. And that was what kept Melanie from hating Alice Hill.

Instead of dwelling on that thought, Melanie turned off the TV, put her things down and peeled Mason from Dawson's arms.

As soon as the weight lifted, Dawson sat up and his hands gripped her arms.

"It's just me," she said quickly, trying not to wake the baby.

Dawson's tight grip released and he rubbed his eyes.

"I'll be right back after I put Mason down," she whispered.

A nod of acknowledgment came, quickly followed by a yawn.

Melanie moved out of the room, her panic mounting. She kissed Mason on the forehead before placing him inside his crib and pulling the covers over him. "Night, my sweet boy."

Facing the man in the next room was even more difficult with her fears mounting. She took a calming breath and marched into the living room.

Dawson was in the kitchen, making coffee.

"Looks like everything went well tonight," she said. Her normal routine had her eating a bowl of cereal, taking a shower and then flopping in bed. Six thirty in the morning would come early and Mason had always been an early riser.

"We got through it," he said, his tone unreadable as he watched the coffee brew. He turned to her. "Did you notice anything strange at work?"

"No. It was a typical Thursday. We actually do a pretty good business. Kicks off the weekend."

"You work every weekend?"

The coffee finished brewing. She handed him a mug, which he immediately filled.

"Yep. Every Thursday, Friday and Saturday night. Working a weekday is the only way I could get a mostly weekend schedule. Money's good so pretty much everyone wants weekends." Melanie pulled out her late-night snack supplies, Cheerios and milk. She made a bowl of cereal and settled on one of the beige bar stools. "Which gives me Sunday through Wednesday on a normal sleep schedule with Mason."

"Is there anyone else around to depend on? Friends?" he asked, taking a sip.

"I don't have time," she said quickly. Too quickly. "I have my sister to keep me company if that's what you're asking. It doesn't seem to be the same for you, but getting the hang of parenting wasn't so easy for me. I don't do anything besides take care of my son."

Dawson seemed to contemplate that with a look of… relief?

"What time does he wake up?" he asked.

"Six thirty."

"In the morning?"

"Afraid so." She took a bite of cereal and chewed. "Which is why I need to finish eating and shower so I can get to bed."

"That's only three hours of sleep if you're lucky," he said in horror.

"Tell me about it," she said. "We take a nap together after lunch. I try to store up as much sleep as I can on my days off to make up for it."

"It doesn't seem healthy for you or him," he said, and she picked up on something in his voice. Admiration?

Nah. She was hearing what she wanted.

"Thanks for being concerned, but it's actually much easier now that he sleeps through the night. How did he feel, by the way? Any sign of the fever coming back?"

"No. He did fine."

"Good." All her worrying had been for nothing. Was it wrong that a little selfish piece of her wanted them to need her help? She finished the rest of her cereal as Dawson leaned against the counter and drained his coffee mug.

"This is normally when I grab a few hours of sleep," she said after placing her bowl in the dishwasher. "I'm sorry that I don't have a guest room. I'm told the couch is comfortable, though."

"Don't worry about it. I've slept all I'm going to tonight."

"Are you sure?"

He nodded.

"Suit yourself," she said. "I need my beauty sleep. My alarm will go off far too soon."

"Tell me what to do and I'll take care of Mason while you sleep in," Dawson offered, pouring another cup.

"Thanks for offering, but Mason thrives on routine. If he doesn't see me first thing, it could be a rough day." Maybe that was hopeful. He and Dawson seemed to get along fine without her before.

"It's high time I became part of that routine, don't you think?" He pinned her with the way he glared at her.

There was no good comeback to that, so she nodded, fought back tears and said good-night.

The warm water from the shower sluiced over her, soothing the tension in her shoulders. Part of her was glad that Dawson was in her apartment under the circumstances. He made her feel physically safe and no one would watch over Mason more closely. And yet his presence brought on a whole new set of issues, too. No matter how much she fought it, she was still attracted to the guy. Plus, there was the complication of him knowing about Mason.

Had Melanie really believed she'd be able to keep this secret forever?

If she were being honest with herself, the answer was no.

Maybe it was good that they were facing this now. They were both reasonable adults and they could surely come up with a compromise that didn't suck the life out of her.

On that note, she finished washing, dried herself and then dressed in her normal bed clothes of boxer shorts and an old T-shirt from college, keenly aware of the male presence in the next room.

Had Dawson been fishing to see if she had a boyfriend earlier? Why did it embarrass her so much to discuss it with him?

There were other priorities in her life at the moment. Maybe she should have turned the tables and asked about his personal life. Lisa and Samantha had kept pretty quiet about his activities in the past few years and Melanie kept herself from asking about him. She knew there was no good that could come out of knowing about his business because he'd moved on.

Speaking of Lisa, Melanie needed to phone her friend tomorrow with an update. If she heard about the break-in, she would be worried. News would most likely travel quickly.

Her pulse picked up.

The whole town would know Melanie's secret soon enough. And she'd have to face Alice Hill.

Tossing and turning for a good hour, Melanie finally let go enough to fall asleep.

MELANIE BLINKED HER eyes open. The sun blared through her window.

What time was it?

The clock read one fifteen, but that couldn't be right. She listened for sounds coming from the next room as she peeled covers off and slipped into her warm-up pants.

Had she forgotten to set her alarm last night? No way. She distinctly remembered doing it.

A moment of panic seized her. What if something had happened to Mason? Or Dawson? She barreled toward the door. The fact that the house was quiet didn't sit well.

There was no one in the living room or kitchen. Mason's room was empty as was the hall bath.

Melanie tore out the front door to see if her car was still there. It was parked right where she left it. Her pulse raced.

Could something have happened?

Wouldn't she have heard a noise?

Maybe her neighbor heard something. She broke into a run, panic pressing down on her chest, making it difficult to breathe. Nothing could happen to her little boy.

Mr. Patterson opened on the second round of knocking, midknock.

Melanie pulled her arm back. "Have you seen Mason?"

The older gentleman gave her a disapproving once-over.

"No. Sure heard him last night, though," he said.

"I'm sorry, what?"

"Could hardly hear my TV for all the crying noise." His nose wrinkled as if he'd tasted something sour.

Had Dawson lied about how well the night had gone? Why would he do that?

Melanie thanked her neighbor, deciding now was not the time to remind him how many times his TV had been turned up so loud that it had disturbed Mason. Instead, she promised it wouldn't happen again. She hoped it wouldn't, at least. Those first few months had been rocky, but she'd figured out plenty of tricks to keep her son calm since then. Sickness or pain couldn't be helped, though. She wished for thicker walls.

Maybe when Mason went to school and she got a better job she'd be able to afford to rent a small house somewhere?

In the meantime, she needed to find her son.

As she turned to go find her cell phone, she heard Mason's laughter. She moved to the parking lot and realized where it was coming from—the playground. Her complex had a small area with a slide and a few swings.

Well, now she was just angry.

She stalked over to the source of Mason's joy, stopping when she saw Dawson smack himself in the head with one of Mason's toys.

Mason roared with laughter.

"What are you thinking taking my son outside without letting me know?" she said, maintaining as calm a voice as she could muster so as not to upset Mason.

"Mama!" Mason exclaimed.

She walked over and kissed his head while the swing stopped. Dawson didn't immediately say anything.

"You're going to give yourself a concussion with that

thing," she said to Dawson, moving behind Mason to give his swing a push.

The boy giggled, clapping his hands. He loved the swings.

"What, this?" Dawson bopped his head again.

Mason laughed so hard he could barely breathe. Melanie giggled. She wasn't thrilled about it, but she couldn't help herself. A grown man smacking himself in the head with a fire engine was funny.

"Is that how you finally stopped Mason from crying last night?" she asked, giving Mason's seat another shove.

"Confession?" he asked.

"Fine. Go ahead," she said, knowing that meant she'd have to forgive him for whatever came out of his mouth next.

"Last night didn't go so well," he said, sounding defeated.

"Why didn't you tell me?" she asked.

"I didn't want you to worry. And I didn't want you to think you had to bring in his babysitter tonight. We survived and I know I can do this," he said quickly.

"Not without being honest with each other." Didn't those words taste bitter?

Especially when Dawson shot her a look and said, "Like you have been with me?"

Okay, he had her on that point. She wouldn't deny that.

"I can't change the past, Dawson. I'm sorry for how everything turned out. I should've trusted you and I was scared." She didn't want to tell him the rest just yet. Not in front of Mason. "We both have adjustments to make if this is going to work. For starters, you can't take the baby without telling me. I was frantic."

"You didn't see my note?" he asked. "I tacked it to

the fridge. Figured you'd get a Pepsi first thing when you got up."

That was actually really thoughtful. She was too busy running around the house like a crazed woman to see it.

"All I did was blast through the place looking for you and Mason. When I didn't hear or see anyone, I panicked." The swing came back a little too fast and hit her arm. "Ouch."

Mason roared with laughter.

"I won't do this again without telling you first. But the same goes for you. I want to know where my son is and what he's doing at all times," he said, firing back.

He made sense. It would be impossible to keep each other updated every second. Wow. This was going to be more difficult than she'd thought. And she hadn't figured it would be a picnic before.

"Leaving a note was the right thing to do," she conceded. "We'll figure it out over time. We're both new at this sharing thing. And you do seem to be doing a good job with him."

"It was dicey until I figured out that me being in pain cracks him up," he said, and she appreciated his attempt to lighten the mood.

"I had no idea he was such a masochist," she said, doing her best to calm down.

"Apparently so." Dawson gave another push.

"I wonder if we should be worried," she joked.

Dawson's half smile tightened a coil low in her belly. It had been too long since she'd been with a man. Suddenly she realized that she must look a mess, and embarrassment heated her cheeks.

Or was the flush caused by something else? Something more primal that accompanied being this close to Dawson?

Chapter Eight

Dawson didn't mean to sound the alarm for Melanie earlier. He'd left a note. The panicked look on her face was the same he felt every time he thought about what had happened to Bethany and the gene he might've passed on to Mason.

Alexander disease might be a rare genetic disorder, but it was a devastating one, taking away everything about Bethany until it had drained her life, too. A burst of anger exploded in his chest as he thought about the past. Sitting on the sidelines with Bethany had him watching a slow death of the brightest star. There'd been nothing he could do to stop it or make it better.

Did Melanie have the same fear?

"Has he been tested?" He studied her, waiting for a reaction.

"No." She looked at him apologetically.

"Have you considered it?" he pressed.

She nodded but didn't speak, and that pretty much told him she didn't want to think about it even though she had.

"When did you feed him lunch?" she asked, and he realized why she was redirecting the conversation. She wouldn't want to discuss something that important in front of Mason.

And she was right. They could talk about it once they got through the weekend.

Dawson checked his watch. "At about twelve. He seemed hungry, so I gave him Cheerios and I cut up bananas. He seemed to really like those."

"I'm impressed. How'd you figure that out?" she asked. He shouldn't allow himself to feel a sense of pride.

"First, I checked in the cabinets. Then I searched my portable nanny here." He held up his phone.

"Of course."

"To be honest, the first thing I looked for was peanut butter and jelly. Thought I'd make him a sandwich."

"His pediatrician wants us to wait until he's at least two. There are so many food allergies now," she said. Then added, "It's about time for an *n-a-p*." She spelled out the last word. "You were so insistent on figuring out everything on your own last night that I didn't warn you how hard it is to put him to bed."

"I deserved that." He could be man enough to admit that.

Melanie gave her son, *their* son, a five-minute warning that they would have to leave the playground.

"I'm guessing the *b-a-t-h* went okay."

"No drama there. The tears didn't start until I tried to dress him after."

"Let me guess. He threw off his clothes and ran down the hallway naked?" Her laugh was musical and Dawson didn't want to notice those little details about her anymore.

"He usually does that?"

"I call him The Streak for a reason. We have a whole thing that we have to go through to get him to bed without him feeling like the world is ending. When I saw you guys on the couch, I worried he might've given you a hard time," she said. "You were so quick to push me out the door last night that I figured you had a handle on it."

Dawson had a lot to learn about his son. He glanced up at Melanie and saw the brightest smile on her face.

Hold on a damn minute. He recognized that look.

"You're gloating," he said.

"Am not," she denied with a twinkle in her eye.

"Are, too," he said. And didn't this argument take him back to their childhood? They'd fought like brother and sister, fierce yet forgiving, except that was where the familial similarities ended. Dawson had never thought of Melanie like a sister.

"Prove it," she countered, and then gave Mason a three-minute warning.

"Challenge accepted," he teased. They both needed a light moment. Even though his heart belonged to his son, becoming a parent overnight was a lot to process. Between that and the very real threat they faced, Dawson could use some levity.

"Time's up, little man," she said.

Dawson steadied himself for the screaming fit sure to come because Mason looked pretty darn comfortable on that swing.

"Are you ready to race?" she asked her son while holding her arms out. Mason's face lit up.

Damn, she was good at this parenting thing. Dawson reminded himself how much more practice she'd had.

He followed behind them, scanning the perimeter of the playground and then the parking lot as they headed back to the apartment.

They'd had a few good moments on the playground and Dawson hoped to expand on that sentiment as they got to know each other as parents.

"I'll just clean him up and tuck him in," she said, looking at him pensively. The awkwardness returned. "Did you want to…"

"Come here, little buddy," Dawson said, dropping to his knees, realizing after watching Melanie that confidence was half the battle with a toddler.

Mason flew into Dawson's open arms, melting any frustration he had about the change in temperature from Melanie. She'd closed up again based on the tension framing her eyes.

After a nice hug, she and Mason disappeared down the hall, hand in hand.

Dawson got busy in the kitchen. Living alone had given him the skills he needed to get by. He'd fed Mason but skipped eating lunch. Melanie was probably hungry, too.

He should still be furious with her, and that emotion simmered somewhere below the surface. However, putting Mason first meant getting along with the boy's mother. That meant setting Dawson's personal feelings aside, because one look at his son and Dawson knew that his own feelings would take a backseat from now on.

For now, he'd focus on lunch. A trip to the grocery store would come later.

From the supplies on hand, he could heat up bean and cheese burritos.

Melanie came in the room, fresh-faced with her hair pulled up in a ponytail. Dawson tried not to think about the full breasts pressing against her white T-shirt or the soft cotton shorts resting on those full hips—hips his finger had trailed down while he admired her body not that long ago.

Even dressed down she looked incredible. Sexy. And woke all kinds of urges inside him. The sex he'd had since was lackluster by comparison.

Based on his body's reaction to thinking about it he needed to think about something else.

Diapers. Now, there was a subject that could kill a sex drive.

"Why are you smiling?" Melanie asked, entering the small kitchen.

"Already fixed a Pepsi for you." He motioned toward the peace offering on the counter. He didn't want to notice the electricity pinging between them or the sizzle of attraction causing his blood to heat. Instead, he focused on stirring the pot of beans.

"That's really nice of you. Thank you," she said as she moved to the other side of the counter.

"How'd you get him to bed so quickly?" Dawson scanned the hallway, half expecting the tot to come running.

"I told you. He loves his routine," she said.

"Which is?"

"For naps I always wash his face and hands and then we race to the bed."

"I'm picking up on a theme here," Dawson said.

"Yep. He loves to run. The more I make things a game, the less resistance I get. I'm all about making things easier and saving the big battles for the important stuff," she said, then took a sip of her Pepsi.

Sounded easy enough. Dawson could do fun.

"What are you making?" Melanie asked.

"Burritos."

"They smell amazing." She closed her eyes and breathed in the scent.

He should've looked away sooner and not let that heart-shaped face distract him. He didn't. And when she opened her eyes again and smiled at him, he lost himself for a second.

"Oh. Watch out for the burner," she said.

Didn't he feel like an idiot? Standing there, staring at her, he'd burned lunch. Dawson pulled the skillet off the stove, set it in the sink and then withdrew his hand.

He'd gotten distracted and now lunch was ruined.

And wasn't that poetic justice?

MELANIE HOPPED OFF the bar stool and sprang into action, opening the window before the fire alarm went off and woke the baby.

"You need some help in there?" she asked.

"No," was the gruff response.

Dawson wasn't being a jerk. He was embarrassed and she felt bad. She could see that, even though he was still processing things, he was making a huge effort to get along and find some common ground. And maybe that meant he wouldn't show up with court documents requesting full custody when the dust settled from recent crazy events.

And would it be so bad to have a partner to help her bring up Mason? If she were being honest the past couple of years had been lonely.

"I can run out and pick something up. You can't imagine how nice it would be to run an errand while Mason's sleeping," she offered.

His eyebrow went up.

"Don't get me wrong, I'm not complaining about caring for him. He's still the best thing that's ever happened to me."

His other eyebrow hiked.

"I'm just saying that I trust you to stay here with him while I pick up lunch."

"Okay. I'll clean up this mess," he relented, waving his hand around the kitchen.

"Turn that thing into a magic wand and maybe the whole place will be clean by the time I get back," she joked, trying to recover the light mood from earlier. Sure, they were stepping on each other's toes and making mistakes. It had only been a few hours.

Dawson surprised her with a sexy little smirk. And didn't a thousand butterflies release in her stomach when he did? Thoughts of his glorious naked male form crowded her mind. So not a good thing right now.

It was a good time to make an exit before her lack of a sex life had her throwing herself at the man after one cute smile.

She grabbed her keys and made it to the car without giving away her reaction and embarrassing herself. No way did Dawson share the same attraction as she did. Okay, that was a lie. Maybe he still felt a spark. It wouldn't matter. She knew the man better than anyone and he'd never forgive her. Plus, she still wasn't being completely honest with him. She needed to find a way to tell him about his mother. Heck, there was so much to talk about. Where did she even start?

Bringing back fast food was most likely the easiest thing she'd do that day.

She returned with burgers, fries and strawberry milk shakes. His favorites. Hers, too, but she didn't want to think about how much they had in common. Right now she wanted to focus her energy on figuring out why Sprigs had come after her in the first place and on keeping Mason safe.

Dawson didn't smile when she handed over the food, and she figured now that Mason was asleep the questions would begin. Dawson had many. She could tell by his expression, and she'd always been good at reading him.

"How long does he usually nap?" Dawson asked halfway through their meal. He must've been starving to wait this long to speak, especially with the way he cleaned his plate.

"Hour and a half if I'm lucky," she said in between bites. "Thirty minutes if I'm not."

"He's a handful when he's awake," he said.

"I'm not complaining," she said defensively, careful not to give him the impression she couldn't handle this on her own.

"It's *me*, Melanie," Dawson said. "Relax, okay?"

That was half the problem.

"What do you want to know?" She eased back on the beige stool.

"What's his favorite food?"

"Easy. Spaghetti," she said, forcing her shoulders to chill.

"Color?"

"He'll tell you that it's blue, but it's actually green." She hadn't thought about how much Dawson had missed of Mason's life. Sharing him would be difficult, but it hit her that it was the right thing to do for Dawson and her son. The two deserved a chance to get to know each other.

Dawson had been taking everything well so far.

"Why didn't you tell me about him?" Dawson asked.

"I was scared."

He shot her a look that said he recognized BS when he heard it.

"Why didn't you really?"

She shrugged.

"I keep thinking about how I'm going to tell my family," he said.

Melanie must've given him a look without trying to, because he pinned her with his gaze.

"What aren't you telling me?" he demanded.

"It's going to take time to learn everything about him, Dawson," she hedged, trying to redirect the conversation back to a comfortable place. "Maybe it's enough for the two of you to get to know each other. We don't have to do this all in one day, do we?"

"No. Of course not. I have plans to stick around. I know we have a lot to work out and he needs to get used to my presence, but you need to know that I have every intention of being there for my son as he grows up." He must've picked up on her discomfort. "And I want to contribute financially, too."

"No, Dawson—"

"I've already given this some thought. All this stuff—" he picked up a diaper and a toy "—must cost a lot. I understand that you don't want to depend on me, but it's not fair for you to bear the burden alone. I have money saved that's sitting there, doing nothing."

"Money that you've been saving since you were thirteen years old. I can't take any of that money. I'll let you help out with diapers and you're welcome to bring him toys—"

"Let me help you buy a condo or small place outside of town. Nothing fancy."

"No way."

"That way you won't have to depend on me for a check every month. Isn't that what you're worried about?" he asked.

"Well, yes, but—"

"You wouldn't have to be if you let me put a roof over your head," he said.

She was shaking her head, which seemed to make him even more determined.

"How much do you pay here?"

"Nine hundred dollars a month."

"For this?" Shock was written across his wide-open eyes as he glanced around.

"It's a two bedroom, and bigger cities have a higher cost of living," she said defensively.

"Then I can save you even more than I thought. You could cut your hours at the bar and spend more time with Mason," he countered. "That way I'll be helping without you feeling like you're standing at the mailbox every month. It's a win-win."

That thought scared her, excited her and gave her night sweats all at the same time. Dawson would be good for Mason, there was no denying that.

She picked up a French fry and chewed on it.

And it looked as though he planned to be there for the long haul.

He'd made that much clear.

"What about your ranch? You've been dreaming of buying one forever," she said. She couldn't argue with his point that it would make her life easier if all she had to work for was groceries, gas and utilities. Her parents had given her their second car last year, since they were on the road so much, so she didn't have a car payment, which had been another godsend.

"You know what they say. Priorities change when you become a parent. Owning a ranch doesn't seem as important to me as making sure my son has everything he needs."

How could she let Dawson give up his dream? His mother's words wound through her head. *He'll resent you for the rest of his life.*

While Dawson's intentions might be good right now, he hadn't really had time to adjust yet. She didn't want him doing something he might regret later.

"That's a great offer, so please don't take this the wrong

way but I can't agree to that right now." Fear hit her that he'd want to bring Mason around his mother. Dawson might want to be part of his son's life, but his mother was a whole different issue.

Heart racing, Melanie decided to set that thought aside. No way could she deal with Alice, this stalker and the fact that her own life had been turned upside down in a matter of hours.

He folded his arms.

"I just want a little time to think about it. This is a lot for me, too. Don't get me wrong, I'd love to spend more time with Mason. That's not it," she said.

"Then what is? Is it me?"

The way he asked that second question nearly tore her heart from her chest. No. It wasn't him. Yes, it kind of was. Everything was all mixed up and she needed a minute to soak everything in.

"This is a lot to digest, Dawson. One minute, I'm home to support a friend and the next a crazed guy is trying to hurt me and you're here." Did that come out right? "I'm grateful for that last part, don't get me wrong."

Relief eased the tension lines bracketing his mouth.

"Good. I was afraid you were going to ask me to leave," he said.

"I wouldn't be that stupid. Or unfair. I need you. Mason needs you. There's a lot we have to sort out for the long run. Right now we need to figure out what Sprigs is up to. I was home and maybe that's the first time he knew where I was. But he's wanted by the law and I'm shocked he would risk getting caught. His life is on the line. Why come after me at all?"

"I can think of one reason," he said. She didn't like Dawson's ominous tone and she knew exactly what he was about to say. "And we already mentioned it."

"He has nothing to lose," she said under her breath.

The rest of their meal was spent in silence. She was contemplating Dawson's offer and how that might change her and Mason's life.

Mason cried, awake too soon, and Melanie excused herself to tend to him. His curls were tousled, his eyes still sleepy.

She made an excuse about needing to clean in order to keep a little distance between her and Dawson for the rest of the afternoon. Besides, she needed something else to occupy her thoughts, and the place needed a good once-over. That didn't normally happen until one of her days off.

Cleaning usually helped clear her mind.

Except one person kept cycling back in her thoughts... Sprigs.

Chapter Nine

More than a week had passed since the break-in at Melanie's parents' house. The few days off Melanie had spent with Mason and Dawson made her dread going back to work the following night even more. They had only broken the ice in terms of figuring things out, but hope was taking seed.

And as much as she didn't want to admit the fact, since she knew how temporary their situation was, having Dawson around was nice. More than that, actually. It was dangerous because she could get used to it.

The man had become decent at putting Mason to bed without any meltdowns.

Melanie had been able to shower without worrying about much of anything besides how warm the water felt against her skin. She pushed aside errant thoughts of the handful of times she and Dawson had made love under jets like those.

By the time Dawson had finished Mason's nighttime routine, she'd settled on the couch with a magazine. He, too, was fresh from the shower. He wore cotton pajama bottoms that he'd bought and no shirt. Water rivulets rolled down his muscled chest.

Melanie forced herself to look away. What could she say? The man was hot. She could hardly blame her body for reacting when he was close. Images of all the places she'd touched that perfect body of his crowded her thoughts. There was precious little she could do to stop those, too. Fine, some things couldn't be helped. She didn't have to wear it on a billboard, she thought, trying to ignore the heat climbing up her neck, flushing her cheeks.

The lights were low, and she hoped that Dawson couldn't see her reaction.

She was never more aware of how little either of them was wearing. Melanie grabbed a throw pillow and hugged it against her stomach as Dawson joined her on the couch.

Thankfully, he'd taken the other side of it.

"Hold on a second." He held a hand up as he disappeared into the kitchen and then returned with two full wine glasses. "Couldn't find that red you used to like."

"That merlot was so good. What was the name of it?" It had been so long she forgot. She also blamed the memory loss on the fuzzy brain that came with having a baby.

But then, when was the last time she'd relaxed and had a drink?

Melanie took a sip of wine and then set the glass on the coffee table, doing her level best not to think about just how long it had been since she'd really relaxed.

"Do you remember that time we caught your mom sneaking a smoke outside when we came home early from school?" Dawson asked.

"I do. We skipped the pep rally so we could hang out at my house," she said. "I was mortified."

"We learned a valuable lesson, though." He laughed. Really laughed. And the sound was sweet.

"No snooping in anyone's business after that," she said. There was the other time she'd come home early and found her mom passed out. The empty wine bottle on the counter had said everything Melanie needed to know about why her mother was facedown, snoring, on the sofa.

Melanie had never asked about either incident. There'd been a few others. Her mother had made such a show of trying to appear like the perfect family that Melanie didn't have the heart to confront her back then.

"I always wondered if Mom was ever truly happy," she said. Every birthday, every holiday, her mother had put on a nice outfit and a smile. She'd spent most of the time in the kitchen while Melanie's dad watched sports on TV. Same story on the weekends. The most sincere thing was the effort her mother put forth in trying to sell the charade to her daughters.

"Did you ever ask?" Dawson took a sip of wine.

"Are you kidding? That was all I ever knew growing up. It never really occurred to me that we were different. I just thought all families were like that." Although her mother had put up a good front, Melanie wondered if she'd ever truly been happy with her father. Did she ever really laugh? Or talk about something that really mattered?

"Funny how families slip into roles and we don't really ever question them," he said.

"Mostly, I remember polite dinner conversation. Looking back, I remember that if anything bad happened we swept it under the rug." Melanie never thought to expect more.

"Now that you mention it, I don't think I've ever seen your parents disagree in all the years I've known your family," he said.

"They are almost like robots if you think about it."

"You don't think they were existing happily together?" he asked.

"Can you think of one time you actually saw my mother laugh?" she countered. "I mean like really laugh?"

"Guess I never thought about it before. I'm sure I've seen her smile."

"Really smile or polite smile?" There'd been such a vacancy behind her mother's eyes and a hollow quality to her laughter. And then there were the times when Melanie's dad went on hunting trips with his buddies and her mother believed Melanie was asleep. Hearing her mother cry at night had been the worst.

"I guess not." He frowned. "How are they on the road together?"

"Probably as polite as ever," she quipped, trying not to think about just how boring that might be.

"Why do you think that is?" he asked.

"Heck if I know." She shrugged. "My family was never very demonstrative of their feelings. I mean, I know my dad loved me. I think he saw his role as the main provider of the family and Mom was there to take care of the girls. When I think back, there isn't one time I remember seeing my parents hug each other. Isn't that weird?"

"Families are complicated beasts," he said.

"At least we became friends out of the deal," she quipped, trying not to think about just how sad her parent's situation had been.

"How so?" His brow went up.

"Well, I couldn't stand being trapped inside my house, so I decided to bug you instead. My sister was too young, too boring." She tossed the pillow at him.

He caught it.

"Lucky for me." He put on one of those killer smiles and her stomach flip-flopped.

"Yes, it was," she teased, trying to distract herself from the sensual shivers rippling through her, centering heat inside her thighs.

"Like I said." He put the pillow behind his head.

"Hey, give me that back."

"You gave it to me." Another devastating grin.

"Everything in this house technically belongs to me, you know. So that makes you a thief." It was so easy to fall back into their old routine. Getting along had never been a problem.

"No way. It was a gift." He turned to give her another ice-melting smile. "And if you want it back, you have to come over here and take it."

She wasn't falling for that trap again.

The last time he'd pulled that card on her, they ended up in bed together. And it had been without a doubt the best sex of her life, which was why she'd done it more. If she closed her eyes, she could still feel his hands on her, roaming her body. She could still see the expression on his face when he looked at her naked. No one had made her feel so adored or so beautiful. This was not the time for her brain to remind her just how long it had been since she'd had sex. She told herself that she was too tired to think about it most of the time and part of that was true. And if she really wanted to be honest, she'd admit the physical act wasn't even what she missed most. Being held afterward, arms and legs in a tangle. Dawson's strong, male form pressed against her. Waking up to him beside her...

"We can always negotiate a compromise." Dawson scooted over beside her, and her pulse sky rocketed.

"For what?" She tried to steady her breathing. He was so close she could smell that unique scent that was all Dawson.

"You want this pillow, right?"

That pitch-black hair. Those serious dark brown eyes. His strong chin and hawk-like nose. He was so close she could feel him breathe.

Melanie forced her gaze away from Dawson's face, his lips, as heat ricocheted between them.

Try as she might, she couldn't stop her gaze from lowering to the dark patch of hair on his chest. Or following the line down to the waistband of the pajama bottoms he'd bought.

"I missed you, Melanie," he said, and his voice was gravelly.

All she had to do was lean forward a few inches and she'd be able to taste the wine on his tongue.

There were many reasons that would be a bad idea, none of which immediately came to mind.

So she didn't resist when his hand came up to her chin and guided her lips to his. They touched lightly at first. He hesitated. Before either of them could decide this was a bad idea, Melanie leaned into the next kiss.

Parting her lips for him, she slid her tongue inside his mouth.

His fingers closed around the base of her neck and she tunneled hers into his thick black hair.

She melted into his touch.

A quick shift in position and his muscled chest was pressed against her and she could feel his weight on top of her.

Getting lost in that moment was as easy as slipping into a sexy outfit. Everything about it made her feel wanted and like a real woman. Breathing in the masculine and clean scent that was Dawson filled her senses.

And she opened her eyes for just a blink. Just enough time to gain her bearings. She pulled back from the kiss.

Dawson responded, quickly pushing up to a sitting position and following her gaze to the hallway.

Nothing was there.

"Did you see something move?" she whispered.

"No." Dawson was on his feet and to the hallway within a few seconds.

She followed a half step behind. They checked Mason's room, her room and both bathrooms and saw no one.

In fact, Mason was in a deep sleep.

When they returned to the living room, she sat down and took a sip of wine.

"I'm sorry. I'm just so used to being on edge." Was that true? Or was she feeling guilty for enjoying herself? Especially with Dawson?

Dawson returned to his spot at the other end of the couch. "It's okay. You're staying alert and that's a good thing. I'm not sorry, though."

DAWSON WASN'T SURE what the hell had just happened, but it was clear that his hormones could run away when it came to Melanie. And unleash more damn frustrating emotions than he needed to deal with while he sorted everything out.

Complicated. Now, there was a good word when it came to his feelings for Melanie.

For now, it was best to keep a safe distance between them, especially because his body seemed to have different ideas. And sex with Melanie would blow his mind. Again. There was no denying that.

There was more than just the two of them to consider now. And Dawson hadn't even broken the news to his parents yet. In fact, he hadn't told anyone from Mason Ridge where he was or what he was doing. In part because he didn't want to take a chance word would somehow get to Sprigs that he was with Melanie or that they had a child.

So far, they'd been safe keeping things quiet. This situation couldn't last forever. Dawson had a life to get back to in Mason Ridge. He had work and friends. Family.

Speaking of his family, he didn't want to tell his parents about his son until he knew for certain that Mason was going to be okay. If he suffered the same fate as Bethany, it would destroy them both. And he needed to bring up genetic testing with Melanie.

So far, his thoughts kept winding back to that kiss and he didn't want to spoil tonight with serious discussion. They'd made good strides toward approaching how they might coparent Mason.

Was he still hurt that she hadn't trusted him enough to tell him when she got pregnant? Hell, yes.

If she'd told him back then, she wouldn't have had to go through all this alone. And he still hadn't gotten her to tell him the real reason she hadn't shared the news.

Melanie had a stubborn streak longer than the I-35. And he was trying not to let that get in the way of their tenuous friendship.

Besides, spending the past week getting to know his son had been right up there with the best of his life.

"I should get some rest," Melanie said.

"You sure about that?" he said. "You barely touched your wine."

"There's no way I can drink the whole glass," she admitted.

"You don't have to. You've never been a big drinker."

"Well, having a baby and working in a bar would've cured me if I had been."

"In that case, I bought playing cards." He set his glass next to hers. "I'm more of a beer and barbecue guy anyway."

Dawson had his work cut out for him. No way could he spend 24/7 with Melanie and have his body not remind him just how desirable she was every time she moved.

Cards might distract him and help keep his hormones under control.

Then again, seeing her full breasts pressed against that white T-shirt made him want to say to hell with silly games.

Chapter Ten

Last night had stirred up all kinds of conflicting feelings for Melanie. The dust would settle soon, law enforcement would find Sprigs and she'd be able to get back to her normal routine. She'd been thinking a lot about Dawson's idea and she couldn't let him give up his dreams so easily.

Facing facts, she needed his help and she understood that a man like Dawson would see it as his duty to contribute both financially and as a hands-on father. She could live with that and, bottom line, the help would be welcomed. As it was, she and Mason lived paycheck-to-paycheck. Without her parents' occasional monetary gift, she wouldn't stay afloat.

Shooting down help would be stupid and selfish. The money would help Mason. What mother didn't want to give her child every possible advantage?

Traffic was heavier than usual on her drive to work, which gave her plenty of time to think about the ways in which she would be comfortable allowing Dawson to contribute. She would most likely still keep her Thursday through Saturday night shifts at the Phoenix Bar. It was only three nights a week and she made good money. Besides, her boss wouldn't let her cut her days back anymore. She already had the best shifts and there'd been grumbling from some of the waitresses with more seniority.

Also, Mason would enter preschool in another year and a half and then she could work more traditional hours in an office setting with paid insurance. Nothing had to drastically change now that Dawson was in their life. If he contributed financially, she'd be able to give their son some extras that she hadn't been able to so far. She'd be able to afford to do more things with him on her days off, like take him to the zoo.

Mason loved animals, and she planned to get her son a puppy some day when she could afford to get a little house with a backyard.

Her typical twenty-minute commute had turned into forty-five. She was relieved when she finally arrived and could slip into her role serving drinks rather than spend any more time getting inside her head about recent events. Besides, the music was far too loud inside the bar to think clearly anyway.

It was usually all too easy to block out the world, getting lost in the rush of shuffling drinks. Except, tonight, Melanie's thoughts kept bouncing back to Dawson and that kiss from last night.

The evening wasn't off to a good start, but by midnight it was elbow-to-elbow and she'd broken a sweat. Those were always good tip nights.

Another hour and a half flew by and, thankfully, it was getting close to quitting time. The crowd was in full swing, a typical Thursday night, which often turned out to be more lucrative than the weekends.

Melanie grabbed her order, a pair of Heinekens for the guys at table three, when the lights blinked, the music blared, and on top of it came a piercing sound.

The fire alarm.

Her heart raced. Everyone had to get out. As Melanie

pushed through the crowd making their way to the exits, she felt a hand on her arm.

Her blood chilled.

No way.

It couldn't be him. Could it?

She wheeled around, preparing to face down the man who she'd tried to avoid for years, whose name brought fear descending around her...who seemed determined to stalk her.

The pressure on her arm eased before she could get a good look at who was behind her. Her heart pounded. Was he there? Was Jordan Sprigs somewhere in the crowd?

Melanie pulled her cell from her front pocket and clamped her fingers around it.

As she moved with the crowd, she pressed Dawson's name on her contacts. The air inside the bar felt as if it had thinned and her chest squeezed from panic.

At least there were plenty of people around. She should be fine if she stayed with the crowd.

"Hello?" Dawson's sleepy voice slid through her, calming her. "What's going on? I hear sirens."

"Fire alarm went off, so we're literally being pushed out of the building by the crowd."

"Get in your car and drive home now." Dawson's voice was too calm, and that was exactly how she knew just how concerned he truly was.

"I can't. My purse is locked in my manager's office."

"Find him. Have him unlock the door and turn over your belongings."

"There's no way," she said. "There are dozens of people jammed in the parking lot."

"Stay near the front door, then," he said. "When we hang up, I want you to call a cab. We can go back for your stuff tomorrow."

"Okay. I'm with a huge crowd of people and I'm right in the middle of them." She didn't share the part where she believed Sprigs had had his hand on her arm. There was nothing Dawson could do from her apartment, she realized, and it probably wasn't him anyway.

"I hear the sirens in the background. Fire department?" he asked.

"Yes. I see the trucks."

"On second thought, stay on the line with me."

"Okay." She talked to him for a few minutes. By the time the firemen cleared the building, which they did remarkably fast, it was past closing time.

"Keep me on the line as you get your purse," Dawson insisted.

"I need to close out first. I'll call you back as soon as I walk out to my car." Melanie tucked her phone in her apron as she followed her fellow employees inside to finish up work and retrieve her bag.

She scanned the parking lot, searching the faces for Sprigs. Then again, he could've sent someone. Any one of them could be working for him.

Her manager, Joel, stood at the open office door. The lights were back on, the room bright, and the crowd was beginning to thin outside.

Once she was safely inside her sedan, she would breathe easier.

Melanie quickly counted her tips and then tipped out the bartender and the busboy who'd worked her station.

"I have babysitter issues and need to get home," she said to Joel. "Will you watch and make sure I make it to my car?"

"Sure thing." Joel pushed back from his computer. He was in his late thirties, had a daughter in kindergarten and saw it as his personal responsibility to make sure those who worked for him made it home safely every night. "How's the lot?"

"Looks like it's emptying out," she said.

Occasionally, one of their customers thought it would be a good idea to hang around and wait for one of the waitresses. There was no shortage of attractive women working, and some men mistook friendly service for something else entirely.

Joel stood at the front of the building, arms folded, as Melanie crossed the lot. She knew to park under a light and felt safer knowing her manager kept watch as she navigated to her vehicle.

There were pairs of people dotted around the lot, standing next to cars. Melanie's nerves hummed as she quickened her pace. She'd call Dawson as soon as she got inside the car and talk hands-free on the twenty-minute ride home.

There were three couples in between her and her car. The odds one of them worked for Sprigs might be low, but adrenaline pumped through her anyway. Hair pricked on her neck and a foreboding feeling trickled ice down her spine. *Joel is watching. It will be fine.*

She used her remote to unlock the car door as she approached, keeping an eye on the pair of people who were huddled close together near a truck four spaces over. Even if one did make a move toward her, she could be inside her car before anyone could reach her.

Melanie wasted no time closing the distance to her vehicle. She turned and waved to Joel. He stood there, waiting for her to back out of the lot.

Dawson picked up on the first ring. "Tell me you're in the car."

"I am," she reassured him, relief washing over her. "I'm about to pull out of the lot."

"Check your rearview. Make sure no one seems too interested in what you're doing or is following you."

Melanie hadn't thought about that. He was right. She wasn't out of the woods yet. She scanned the area behind her. "So far, so good."

There was so much tension coming through the line.

"How about now?" he asked. His voice was a study in focus and she appreciated the sense of calmness moving through her.

"A truck just turned out of the lot and is heading toward me." Her pulse ratcheted up a few notches and her palms warmed.

"Keep an eye on him and let me know if he gets too close. Are you on State Street?"

"Yes. I'm coming home the way I showed you," she said.

"Good. Don't veer from that course unless I say."

"Okay." The light changed and she pressed the gas a little harder than she'd intended to, jerking forward.

"Melanie?"

"Sorry. I'm fine. Just a little nervous." She must've made a sound without realizing.

"You're doing great. Take a deep breath."

She did, making it through the next few lights with ease. It helped that they were green.

The light turned red in the next block. Her shoulders knitted together with tension as she came to a stop and the truck engine whirred behind her.

"Now check your rearview," Dawson said. "See anyone you recognize?"

Melanie strained to get a good look at the driver.

"It's a woman." Relief flooded her. This was racking up to be one heck of a long night.

"A few more lights and you'll be on the highway," Dawson said. "And then you'll be home in another ten minutes."

"Getting home and taking a long, cool shower never sounded better," she said, glancing in her rearview.

"I'll have the water running for you," he said.

The truck's turn signal came on.

"She's about to turn," Melanie said.

"Any other cars out?"

"None that I can see," she said.

"Good. You'll be home free soon." Dawson's voice sounded hopeful.

And that made her feel incredibly optimistic.

"Done. She just turned and disappeared."

"Any other activity around you?"

"None. It's quiet. And dark. I'm about to pull up to another red light, but it looks good so far." A sprig of happiness sprouted inside her.

Foot on the brake, she tapped her finger on the steering wheel. She was so ready to be home. A bowl of Cheerios sounded better than steak right now.

Suddenly, a noise sounded from the backseat and a hand came over her mouth. She tried to scream, but only a muffled cry came out.

A dark figure emerged from behind.

"Melanie?" Dawson sounded concerned.

She tried to shout his name, yell for help, but the hand tightened, making it impossible to form words.

"Melanie?" This time, Dawson sounded stressed.

The call disconnected.

"He can't help you now."

Melanie would recognize that voice anywhere… Sprigs.

She had a half second to think and no bright ideas

came, so she jammed her foot on the gas pedal. She'd bite his hand if she could, but he'd secured a gag over her mouth. *Oh God, no.*

"Brake," Sprigs demanded. His sinewy voice was not more than an inch from her right ear. Her skin crawled where he breathed on her.

Despair pressed heavily on her shoulders. All she could think about was Mason and his father. She was grateful for the crash course she'd given him in taking care of their son, because if Sprigs had his way, she wouldn't be around to do it herself. *Son of a bitch.*

"I said get your damn foot off the gas," Sprigs repeated, high-pitched and angry, leaving no room for doubt how serious he was. "I'll slit your throat right now."

A hard piece of metal pressed against her throat. A knife?

The reality of the situation hit fast and hard. He wanted to kill her? She shook her head. She might not make it out of this alive, but neither would he. No way would she let him walk away and hurt more kids.

He'd die with her.

Melanie slammed the steering wheel a hard right, popped the curb and aimed the front end of her car toward a brick office complex.

Flooring the pedal, she jabbed her elbow into his face to back him off her as much as she could, praying the object pressed to her neck didn't slice through her skin.

His head bucked and he slammed his hand into the back of her headrest.

"Dammit," he said. "Hear me now. If you'd listened to me before, we wouldn't be in this situation in the first place."

Melanie turned her head to the side, closed her eyes and braced for impact.

"Take your foot off that pedal." Agitated, his voice rose again.

I love you, Mason.

Chapter Eleven

The blunt pressure on Melanie's neck eased a few seconds before the air bag deployed and her body lurched forward. Sprigs had to have dropped to the floorboard, because without a seat belt he'd most likely be dead with an impact like that one.

Everything went blurry, dizzy and she was confused, trying to process what had just happened. Seconds ticked by. Or minutes. She couldn't be sure which.

Still dazed, she felt her instincts kick in and she managed to curl her fingers around the door handle and then push the door open with her left shoulder. She spilled out onto the concrete and fell onto all fours, heaving.

There was no time to waste. Everything in her body screamed to run, to get out of there and as far away as possible. Her thoughts immediately jumped to her son and holding him again. An image of him safe with his father pushed its way through her mind, powering her body to move forward. And Dawson.

Hope blossomed as she scrambled to her feet and then took off.

At any moment and with every step she expected a hand to grab her, jerking her back. So she pushed harder.

Because the only other thing she could think about was how much Mason needed his mother and maybe his father needed her just a little bit, too. She told herself it was because there was so much she needed to share with him about their son, but immediately she knew it for the lie it was.

When she was about to clear the block, she glanced back, needing to know if Sprigs was right behind her.

He wasn't. There was no sign of him.

Even so, her heart pounded as she bolted around the corner and then down the residential street. She could hear highway noise in the distance. That was how close she'd been and that was most likely the reason Sprigs had acted when he did.

Dawson must be frantic with worry after their call had been cut off. Dawson. A piece of her heart broke knowing Dawson would never trust her again.

It was the middle of the night and there were no lights on in the row of bungalow-style houses. Thankfully there were no dogs barking, either. At least not at the moment.

How had Sprigs found her?

It didn't matter. He had and now she had to figure out a way to get help and call police.

Stopping to knock on a door was risky. It could give Sprigs time to catch up, especially if he was getting close or coming at her from another angle.

Legs burning, Melanie slowed down and scanned the street behind her. It was too dark to see clearly, so she watched for any signs of movement.

Both sidewalks and the street seemed clear. She double-checked front lawns. Didn't see anything there, either. It was too soon to breathe easy.

Thank the heavens for her seat belt and for air bags. She'd been dazed but she'd made it out alive. Surely Sprigs was unconscious or worse. Was it too much to hope the nightmare could end? That he didn't survive the crash?

At the very least, he'd been slowed down and she'd escaped. And that was worth something. Tears streaked her cheeks and she didn't have the energy to fight them.

Thinking about injuries, Melanie had no idea if she'd been hurt during the accident. There'd be time to evaluate any scrapes and bruises later. Everything felt numb. No doubt she was still in too much shock to make a real determination.

For now, she could run and had no pain.

If she waited too long to knock on a door, she might be giving Sprigs time to catch up or disappear. Part of her needed to keep running. To put as much distance between she and Sprigs as she could to make sure he couldn't get to her.

On the next block, she stopped at the first door and knocked. A tiny, high-pitched, rapid-fire bark sounded on the other side.

Another dog barked two houses down. And then across the street.

Melanie bit back a curse and prayed like the dickens that Sprigs was knocked out and not searching the streets for her. If he was, he'd no doubt find her thanks to the noise.

She banged on the door again, louder this time, and a light came on. The little dog was going crazy barking.

Melanie could feel her heartbeat in her throat as the door swung open. A sturdy man, midthirties, glared at her from the other side.

"I'm so sorry to bother you, but it's an emergency. There's been an accident." The words rushed out as a flood of tears released. She glanced around, searching for signs of Sprigs. "May I use your phone? Please."

The big guy checked around her as if he half expected someone to jump out from behind her, and then nodded.

"Thank you." Melanie opened the screen door and repeated those two words.

"Who is it, Roger?" A female wearing a time-worn cotton bathrobe emerged from the hallway. Her short dark hair stuck out at odd angles.

"Go back to bed, honey. I'll take care of it," Roger said.

"I'm so sorry to disturb you, but I've been in an accident and there was no one…" A sob tore from Melanie's throat. She suppressed the next one. "I didn't know what to do so I ran here."

No way could she tell them more or let her guard down, not with Sprigs still out there. Even though Roger looked capable of handling himself.

"Are you all right?" the woman asked, picking up the barking dog and shushing it.

Melanie nodded through sobs as Roger flipped on the living room light.

The woman gasped. "Your arms. You're hurt."

"Celia, get a wet towel," Roger said.

"I'm fine. I just need to use the phone," Melanie said, glancing down for the first time. Her arms were bloodred from what looked like burn marks. She didn't have time to worry about them. Burns would heal. She needed to call the police and then let Dawson know that she was okay. "And please don't answer the door if anyone knocks."

"Sit down." Roger pointed to the plaid sofa with a severe look on his face. "I'll get my cell."

By the time he returned, Celia was by Melanie's side, gently pressing the towels to her forearms.

"You said you were in a crash?" Roger said, handing over the phone.

Melanie nodded.

"Anyone else with you?" he asked.

Melanie hesitated. Tell the truth and what would happen? Would Roger go check on the other person?

Lie and she'd get caught. She had to tell the dispatcher who was in the car with her.

"Yes." More sobs released as Melanie called 9-1-1. She didn't realize how badly she was shaking until just now.

"What is your emergency?" the operator asked.

"I was just in a car crash near Northwest Freeway Highway 290," Melanie said.

"Do you need an ambulance, ma'am?" the dispatcher asked, her voice a calming force in the chaos churning through Melanie.

"I don't think so. I was attacked by a man named Jordan Sprigs and that's the reason I wrecked. He's wanted by the FBI and I think he's still at the crash site." Panicked, she glanced up at Celia and then Roger, who were passing a look between them, and Melanie's heart skipped a beat.

Celia patted Melanie's leg reassuringly.

"Are you there with him now?" the dispatcher asked.

"No. I got out of the car and ran a few blocks to get away. I don't think he followed me. We hit the wall hard, he wasn't wearing a seat belt and I have no idea what condition he's in."

"Okay," the dispatcher said. "Tell me what happened. An officer is on his way to the scene as we speak."

Melanie caught a glimpse as Roger and Celia exchanged another worried glance. She heard Celia tell him to lock the door before she whispered that she'd be back as soon as she got dressed.

Roger clicked the lock, and then disappeared down the hall as Melanie recounted the events to the dispatcher.

It had all happened so fast that Melanie couldn't remember all the details, but she drew the best picture she could of the timeline.

Celia returned wearing warm-ups. Her hair had been brushed.

"Can we turn off the lights?" Melanie asked after ending the call. "Just in case he's wandering around looking for me?"

Celia nodded, complied immediately. There was still a glow coming from the electronics and soft wall lights in the room. They provided enough light to see. Celia came over and sat next to Melanie on the couch.

"How are those arms?" she asked.

"Honestly, I don't think the shock has worn off. I can't feel anything."

"We should put something on them," Celia said, her brow creased with worry. "Burn salve."

"Do you mind if I call my boyfriend?" For lack of a better term. "We were on the phone when it all happened and he must be climbing the walls by now."

Roger returned with a twelve-gauge shotgun resting on his arm.

"Go ahead," Celia said. "Can I get you anything else? Water?"

"No. Thank you." Melanie punched in Dawson's number.

He answered on the first ring.

"It's me. I'm okay," she said immediately.

"What happened?" He didn't bother to hide the stress in his voice now.

"He was in the car. In the backseat," she said, tears streaming down her cheeks.

"Sprigs?"

"Yes," she said, taking a gulp of air. She reminded herself that she was okay and to breathe.

"Where are you?" Dawson asked.

"I'm at a nice couple's house. They let me in." Sirens sounded in the distance and Melanie's shoulder slumped forward. For the first time since the ordeal happened, she felt Sprigs couldn't get to her.

"What's the address? I'm coming right now." No matter how determined he seemed, she couldn't let him bring their son anywhere near this place.

"Don't wake Mason. I'm safe. No one can hurt me now. The police are on their way and they'll get him this time," she said in between gulps of air.

"How'd you get away from him?" Dawson asked.

"I crashed the car into a building," she said quietly, ignoring the gasp that came from Celia.

"You did what?" Dawson's voice was incredulous.

"There was no other way to get away from him, so I slammed my foot on the gas pedal and aimed for the nearest building," she said.

"Melanie, are you sure you're okay?" Dawson lowered his voice and his pain was a knife ripping through her chest.

"I did what I had to, Dawson. He didn't hurt me, but he intended to and I knew it." Her voice hitched no matter how strong she was trying to be.

"I know he did, sweetheart. I'm just grateful that you're alive." His voice was so anguished her heart burned.

"He didn't hurt me," she repeated. "And as soon as I give my statement to police, I'm coming home."

For the first time since this whole ordeal had started, she believed those last three words.

"Yes, you are," he said. "And then we're getting the hell out of here."

"Okay." He was right. Sprigs at the very least knew the area in which she lived. It wouldn't be long before he figured out her address, if he didn't already know. She couldn't take any chances when it came to Mason. And she had every intention of living long enough to watch all the milestones he had yet to achieve.

Squad car lights blared outside. A few seconds later, a knock sounded at the front door.

"I better go, Dawson. The police are here."

"Can I speak to the owner of the house?" he asked.

"Sure." She glanced at Roger and moved the phone from her ear. "He'd like to talk to you."

Roger was already at the door when he nodded. He invited the officer inside and then took the phone from Melanie.

Adrenaline must be wearing off, because Melanie started shaking even harder. Celia dabbed aloe on Melanie's arms and then put a blanket over her legs as the officer introduced himself as Special Agent Randall. He asked a few questions as she accepted a glass of water from Celia.

"Is he still there?" she asked Special Agent Randall once initial information had been relayed. "Did they catch him?"

"I'll check." He took a couple of steps toward the door and asked through his radio if the suspect was in custody.

Melanie held her breath waiting for the answer to come. Sprigs had to be there. Otherwise he would've followed her. Right?

She heard the officer thank the responder as he moved near her again.

"He must've fled the scene. Officers are searching for him and we've notified our FBI liaison," Special Agent Randall said.

No. This couldn't be.

"How could he survive that impact?" she asked, still stunned.

"He might've crawled a few hundred yards away into the brush or managed to get into a Dumpster to hide. If he's around here, we'll do our best to find him, ma'am."

Those words, meant to be reassuring, left a hole in Melanie's chest. As long as Sprigs was out there, she'd have to watch every shadow. She'd have to expect him around every corner. She'd have to fear closing her eyes.

And, worst of all, she was afraid he could get to Mason.

The thought sent an icy chill racing down her spine.

"Thank you," she said, tamping down her worst fears. "Is there any chance my purse or cell phone was found?"

"Both of those items are on their way here right now," Special Agent Randall said.

At least she would get those back. The thought of Sprigs getting away with her personal belongings sent a different kind of chill down her spine, like the feeling people described of what happened when a cat walked over a grave.

The officer finished the interview by letting her know that the city would tow her car for her.

She thanked him again.

"Would you like access to medical treatment?" he asked.

"No. I'm fine," she said, fearing she would never be fine again. Sprigs would see to that.

"Can I offer you a ride somewhere?" Special Agent Randall asked.

"I told her boyfriend that I'd drive her home," Roger said.

That must've been why Dawson had wanted to speak to Roger.

"I can't let you do that. You've already done so much," Melanie said.

Roger shook his head. "It's no trouble."

"We want to help," Celia said. "Don't think twice about it."

"I don't want to burden you guys—"

Roger's hands went up. "I'm a man of my word."

"Thank you both. I don't know what I would've done if you hadn't answered the door when you did." The thought of what Sprigs wanted to do to her made her stomach churn.

He was still out there.

DAWSON HAD ALL the essentials packed up and ready to go by the time Melanie walked through the front door.

She ran straight into his arms, where he hauled her against his chest. He tilted her head back and kissed her on the forehead, each eyelid and then her lips.

The thought that she might not come home had eaten away at his stomach lining.

The past few hours had been pure hell.

"You're safe," he whispered as she trembled in his arms.

Anger ripped through him at the thought of what could've happened to her. She'd been quick on her feet and that was the only reason she was here in his arms and not stranded somewhere with that sick bastard Sprigs, or dead.

Her chin came up and there was defiance in her stare. "I couldn't let him take me. I had no doubt he would eventually kill me when he was through with me. All I could think of was Mason growing up without a mother and how much he needed me."

"You did the right thing," Dawson reassured her. And then he just held her, trying not to notice how much her body molded to his or how warm her skin felt against his own. "Is Roger outside?"

"He left."

"I wanted to shake his hand and give him some money for gas," Dawson said.

"He wouldn't take anything from me. He said to tell you not to worry about it. Said he hoped that if something like that ever happened to his Celia, someone would do the right thing and help her, too."

Dawson was grateful to the man and he would find a way to repay him.

Melanie told him what had happened and showed him the card that Special Agent Randall had given her. It had a phone number she was supposed to call if Sprigs showed up again in addition to a case number scribbled on it.

"Your car is evidence, so I'm sure you won't be getting that back anytime soon and even if you did it won't be drivable. My SUV is still in Mason Ridge, so I figure we'll need a rental," he said.

"He got away, Dawson." Her words trembled as much as her body when she said it.

"Not for long," he said. "Even if he could walk after a wreck like that, he couldn't have gone far. They'll catch him tonight or tomorrow. They want him as much as we do." He doubted that was possible but said the words to offer her some reassurance.

"And if they don't?" She pulled back from him a little, and he repositioned so as not to hurt her arms. Wide, fearful eyes stared up at him.

"They will. If not, then I will. He just made a huge mistake when you got away. One I'm grateful for. It's only a matter of time for him now that they have a general vicinity." Dawson held her tighter, not quite ready to let her go.

"I hope you're right," she said.

She leaned into his chest and for one crazy second the world felt right again. Dawson reasoned that recent events had him off balance, and the thumping in his chest meant nothing more than gratitude that Mason's mother was home safe.

"In the meantime, I'm taking you and our son to my family's lake house," he said.

"Your parents still own that place?"

"They do." Although no one in the family had used it since Bethany was alive. His heart dropped to the toe of his boot and he was filled with the same sense of dread he'd felt when the doctor said all they could do was help her rest comfortably. It had been his idea to take Bethany to the lake house, her favorite place on earth, when she was losing her last little grip on life. It was the last place anyone would ever think to look or expect Dawson to go.

That was precisely the reason it would be perfect for the three of them.

Facing that place again was as appealing as swallowing fire. But Mason and Melanie were the priorities now. And Dawson would do whatever it took to ensure their safety.

"The car rental place doesn't open for another…" Dawson glanced at his watch "…forty-five minutes."

"I just remembered that I don't have a car seat anymore," Melanie said.

"Not a problem. They rent those. I've asked for an SUV with a car seat and GPS. Should we wake Mason?"

"Let's let him sleep. I might as well pack his breakfast." She took a step back and started toward the kitchen.

"Already done," Dawson said. "I had to do something productive to force myself to stop pacing earlier."

Melanie turned around.

"How did he find me, Dawson?" Her chin was defiant, but her voice was small.

"I don't know." If there was a way to keep Melanie and Mason safe tucked away somewhere, Dawson would hunt the son of a bitch down personally and make sure he never hurt another woman or child. As it was, he wouldn't be able to leave them with anyone else or let either of them out of his sight. Not even his best friends in Mason Ridge, and Dawson trusted those guys with his own life.

He thought about calling them for backup and that thought died quickly on the vine.

First of all, he didn't want anyone to know about their new location. He wasn't worried that his friends would tell anyone where he was going. That wasn't the problem. He didn't want to take a chance that anyone could intercept the call.

Another advantage Dawson had at the moment was that Sprigs didn't seem to realize that Dawson was with Melanie and the creep might not know about their son, either. For Mason and Melanie's sake, Dawson needed to keep a lid on his new role as father. All it would take would be one look at Mason and Dawson's friends would make the connection.

Second, all of his friends had been through the wringer in recent weeks while authorities were trying to identify and then arrest those involved with the child abduction ring. Everyone inside Dawson's circle had been touched by recent events, and some of them still had the physical marks to prove it.

"I considered the possibility that he would send someone else after me, but I didn't think in a thousand years that he would come himself. Not when he has this much heat on him," Melanie said. "And how did he get in my car? I promise that I locked the doors before. I always do and I'm being extra careful now."

Sprigs was smart and that made him a helluva lot more dangerous. And deadly.

"I've been thinking a lot about that." Dawson shouldn't notice how beautiful her brown eyes were right now or allow his emotions to take over, because they had him wanting to take her in his arms and never let go. He reasoned that he was still shaken up at the thought of almost losing her. He'd spent a good half hour not knowing what had happened to her and fearing the worst. "He may have gone back to your parents' house and found a pay stub lying around."

"I cleaned my purse out when I was there. All he'd have to do is look through the trash," she said.

"Then my guess is that he pulled the fire alarm to create enough of a diversion to get everyone out of the building."

"He had access to my purse," she said. "But we came right back in and got our things. Someone would've seen him coming in and out if he went outside to unlock my car, wouldn't they?"

"He'd only have to use your remote to unlock your doors," Dawson said.

"So that must mean he was watching me earlier when I arrived at work? Otherwise, how would he know which one was mine?"

"All he'd have to do is click the remote and he could see which car belonged to you. In all that commotion and with the fire alarm blaring, no one would notice what was going on in the parking lot." Dawson paced.

"People were leaving left and right after the alarm," she said.

"He wouldn't have to know which purse was yours, either. All he'd have to do is check wallets for identification. The fire alarm would be the perfect cover. He could've hid inside the bathroom until everyone cleared out. Then, with all the racket of the sirens outside, he'd be able to cover the sound of your car unlocking. Was it busy?"

"The place was packed." Her jaw fell slack. "If he checked my ID then he could've taken my driver's license."

Chapter Twelve

Melanie poured out the contents of her purse and located her wallet. Dawson noticed her hands were still shaking. In that moment, he wanted to put his own hands on Sprigs. Preferably around the man's neck.

"It's here." She pulled out her ID. "And my credit cards, too."

"Anything else missing that has identifying information on it?" He also noticed the burn marks on her arms.

"Everything's here." She gasped. "He might've memorized my address. All it would take is one good look and he could remember where I live."

"Even if he did, he won't come here tonight. Besides, I doubt he can walk after the wreck you described. His body would've taken all the impact while he was down on the floorboards. At a minimum, he's shaken up and has gone into hiding until everything cools down. Best case, he's lying in a ditch somewhere bleeding until the feds pick him up and lock him away for good."

It had taken real courage to do what Melanie had done. She'd done good. Dawson didn't want to be *this* proud of her actions. Denying that he was wouldn't change anything, so he chalked his pride up to their history. "Also, he should realize that the feds will be watching this place from now on, which brings me to another point. I should let them know where we're heading."

"You're probably right. The whole thing just gives me the creeps. I've had a bad feeling ever since his name came up in connection to the child abductions, and I haven't been able to shake it. Even though I shut down everything on social media and cut off ties except to those who I was closest to. I figured he would give up on his fixation with me at some point and just go away or find someone else to put his attention on," she said. "It had been quiet for a few years. Especially since I disappeared and had the baby. Now this—this is all just too close to home, you know?"

He knew there was another reason she'd withdrawn from everyone and it had to do with their relationship.

No way was he about to discuss that. This wasn't the time or place.

"You might want to pull together whatever personal belongings you'd like to have with you," he suggested, ignoring the frustration still fresh in his mind at how easy it had been for her to shut him out.

"And Mason's," she said.

"I packed for him." He had an idea of exactly what she would want to take, but it wasn't his place to rummage through her personal stuff. "Are you hungry?"

"I doubt I could eat anything after everything that's happened," she said.

"You have time to grab a shower before we leave." He would pack something for her to eat on the drive. She needed to keep up her strength.

"That sounds like heaven right now." She started to get up and stopped. Her gaze shifted from the floor to him, and something exploded inside his chest the second she made eye contact. "Dawson, I'm really glad you're here."

"Me, too." He dismissed the feeling.

"I mean it. I can't think of a better friend to have around when the chips are down."

"We've been through a lot together over the years." Dawson half smiled. Most of their trials had come from him during his childhood when she helped him through a difficult time, and he didn't mind returning the favor of being there for her.

"Sure have," she said with a sigh.

"It's my turn to have your back, Melanie. I don't think I ever officially thanked you for being there for me when we were kids."

"You didn't have to say the words. I knew," she said.

He smiled at her as she passed him on her way to the shower, ignoring the sliver of light reaching into the darkest places of his soul.

Dawson studied Special Agent Randall's card while Melanie was in the next room. He retrieved his cell and punched in the number.

The agent picked up on the first ring.

"My name is Dawson Hill and I'm helping my friend Melanie Dixon." He'd used the word *friend* for lack of a better term. Besides, it was true. No matter what else the two of them were or had been, they'd always been friends.

"Ms. Dixon mentioned you." Special Agent Randall introduced himself and then the two exchanged greetings.

That fact should make this call go easier than Dawson had expected.

"What can I do for you, Mr. Hill?" Special Agent Randall asked.

"Any word on Jordan Sprigs?" he asked.

"That's a negative, sir. Sprigs is still at large," Randall said. "We're working with local law enforcement and have a lot of resources invested in his capture. The problem with a man like him is that he can easily disappear into the same outlets he uses to move children."

"I was hoping he wouldn't survive the crash," Dawson admitted, wishing he would have better news for Melanie when she finished her shower. She was already so on edge she'd jump out of her skin if so much as a fly landed on her.

"In all honesty, we all shared that hope," Randall said on a hard sigh. "But he's still out there and we're not giving up until we locate him. We know that he's fixated on Ms. Dixon and that leads us to believe that he won't go far. He'll want to be close to her now that he's pinpointed her location."

"He sent someone to attack her at her parents' house in Mason Ridge a week ago," Dawson said. "I was there."

"I didn't see a report come through on that," Randall said, concerned. "When did you say the incident occurred?"

"It was a week ago. We stayed at a motel that night and then there was a fire the next morning. I'm sure it was him. He has a history with fire," Dawson said.

"The second incident was reported to the task force. The fire marshal's initial assessment is that he suspects foul play. He's continuing his investigation to pinpoint the cause and it'll take a little while to process the scene." Randall's voice had returned to an all-business pitch. "Tell me more about the home invasion."

Dawson relayed the details.

"I'll make contact with the sheriff's department and request that incidents involving you or any of your friends be reported to us immediately," Randall said, his frustration evident in his tone. "Ms. Dixon returning to her childhood home could've been the trigger that caused Sprigs to reignite his fixation on her."

"I'm guessing something in his background must be linked to this behavior, but I didn't know the guy very well," Dawson said.

"Can you tell me anything about him?"

"I know that he kept to himself growing up. I didn't even know he and Beckett Alcorn were friends until all this news broke. In fact, thinking back, I don't remember him having many friends at all."

"Which could've been the first problem," Randall said. "And would also make him easy to manipulate."

Randall made an excellent point. If Sprigs was lonely, had some issues, it could make him pliable. Dawson didn't need to work in law enforcement to put those pieces together. "He was older than us and we pretty much stuck to friendships in our grade. The only reason I knew any of the older boys was my friend Ryan's older brother, Justin. You think Alcorn was pulling the strings on that whole operation?"

"That's what we're trying to figure out," Randall said.

"Does seem hard to believe someone so timid could be the mastermind behind a child kidnapping ring."

"What about family? Did you ever have any dealings with the Sprigses?"

"Not really."

"Were there any rumors about strange behavior?" Randall asked.

"His father died when we were pretty young. Can't say what kind of person he was. Heard that his mom was a religious nut of some kind. I have no idea if that's true or not. He got teased a lot, even by younger kids. The only reason I remember his dad was that traffic shut down on Elder Parkway on the day of his funeral. There was a big game on that day and I overheard older folks complain about the inconvenience. Most people in town are decent, so I remember thinking that Sprigs's dad must've been a jerk. Couldn't say for sure one way or another personally, but it did make me wonder. Can't say I remember much else about the family." Dawson intended to ask around on his own. "Wish I could be more help."

"Alcorn might be the key to putting the pieces together. I have another interview scheduled with him this morning. He's given up his partner, but he's protecting information about their routes, and my guess is that they plan to keep business running as usual. He claims that he wasn't involved in logistics, but my experience tells me that he knows more about it than he's telling us. If we catch Sprigs, we might not need Alcorn's information. Either way, we'll have more leverage when both are in custody."

"Melanie doesn't feel safe here anymore after last night," Dawson said.

"That's certainly understandable under the circumstances," Randall said. "I can arrange protective custody."

"We're planning to leave the apartment and I'd like to move her and Mason to a lake house owned by my family. It's isolated there. No one knows that we own it because we haven't used it in years," Dawson said, figuring this was as good. "She's concerned he has her address after breaking into her car."

"To be honest, we're hoping that's true. I'd like to place a female agent in the apartment in Melanie's absence."

"As bait?" Dawson asked.

"Yes. Can you talk to her and get back to me?"

"She won't mind. She'll do anything to cooperate if it means taking that son of a bitch off the streets."

"Good. That will go a long way toward an end to this," Randall said. "I'll notify my surveillance crew of the change. One thing to consider is that she'll be vulnerable during the transition to the new place. I'd like to offer assistance in transporting her."

"That would be much appreciated." Dawson had been concerned about that, too. No way would he put her and Mason in danger unnecessarily. The extra security measures would help ease his apprehension.

"What's the address?" Randall asked.

Dawson provided it.

"Hold on one second, please." The sound of fingers pounding a keyboard came through the line. Randall must be pulling up the location on his computer. "With one main road leading in and out of the property, we'll be able to control access. However, there are a lot of trees and that could make it more interesting to cover the acreage."

Dawson knew firsthand how easy it was to disappear under the canopy. Even after all these years he remembered the layout. Some of his best times with Bethany had been spent running through those woods. "We had a security system installed out there for the house. It was state-of-the-art at one time. Hopefully that will minimize any concern."

"How about the perimeter? Anything we should know about security-wise there?" Randall asked.

"Barbed wire fencing. Nothing that's hot, though," Dawson said. "My mother didn't want to take a chance either of her kids would have an accident."

"How soon do you plan to leave?" Randall asked.

"I'd intended to wait until a car rental place opened, since my SUV is in Mason Ridge and Melanie's car is no longer drivable," Dawson said. He heard the water turn off in the bathroom and an image of Melanie naked, stepping out of the shower, assaulted him. He shoved the thought aside.

"We can provide transportation," Randall offered.

"How soon can you arrange it?" Dawson figured Melanie would be out soon enough and ready to go. He wondered how long it would be before Mason stirred. Thankfully, his son had been well during the past week other than the occasional cough. Melanie had been right. Mason really did get sick fast and hard, and well just as quickly.

"I can assemble a team in about an hour."

"We'll hold tight until then," Dawson said.

"I'd like to pick up the keys to the new location now and send a couple of guys to sweep the place before you arrive." Randall asked.

"Absolutely." Dawson had no problem agreeing to the extra security measures. While he had no doubt about his own ability to handle Sprigs, Dawson had no idea how many others worked for the man. Besides, he'd cooperate in any way if it meant more security for Melanie and Mason. The hours he'd spent pacing, waiting for her, had been right up there with the worst of his life. And he'd endured doozies. He had no intention of making it easy for Sprigs to get to her, and he had no idea what the crazed man would do to Mason.

Dawson had no plans to risk finding out.

Melanie, dressed in a T-shirt and jeans, walked into the room and sat on the edge of the coffee table near where Dawson stood. He acknowledged her with a nod and then turned his attention to the window. He'd have time to fill her in during the drive. Besides, seeing her fresh-faced from a shower reminded him of the things they liked to do to each other in there, and this wasn't the time to think about it.

Dawson thanked the agent and then ended the call.

Sprigs could be anywhere, even outside at that very

moment. He'd been smart enough to avoid capture so far. The fact sat heavy on Dawson's thoughts.

Sprigs's networks had to be pretty sophisticated to pull off something like this, and he'd gotten away with abducting children for far too many years. Calculating back, Sprigs would have had to begin while he was still in high school and practically still a child himself.

What kinds of horrible things had to happen to a guy to twist him up like that so early in life?

It didn't take long to fill Melanie in on the new plan and bring her up to date with the conversation Dawson had had with Randall.

"I have a lot of questions for him," she said.

"He's planning to meet us at the lake house. Or we could call him back if you'd like."

"It can wait. My nerves are still jumbled and that'll give me time to sort everything out in my head," she said.

"He offered protective custody."

"Won't the lake house be pretty much the same thing?" she asked.

Dawson nodded as he heard Mason cry in the other room. He told Melanie to hold on as he went to his son. Mason wanted down immediately, so Dawson complied. The little guy charged into the next room still half-asleep.

Melanie scooped him in her arms, wincing when he made contact with her burns.

"Want me to take him?" Dawson wasn't being territorial. He wanted to give her a chance to heal.

"No, thanks. I got this." She put Mason in his high chair and then gave him a small bowl of Cheerios while she cut up a banana and poured milk in his special cup.

She sat at the table next to him while he ate; then she wiped his face and hands and drew him to her chest, holding him as though she might never see him again.

Dawson understood why she'd want to do that after her near-death experience. She had to have considered the possibility at some point last night.

"I need to make contact with the guys back home." He needed to check in with his friends in Mason Ridge, who would no doubt start to worry if he didn't show up in town soon. Plus, he wanted to pick their brains about Sprigs.

And there were half a dozen other calls he needed to make to keep his affairs in order as he kept Melanie and Mason safe. Keeping his job had never been more important now that he had a child. Luckily, he'd been saving his vacation days and had another week before he ran out of those. The investigation could take longer and he had no idea what he'd do then. No way was he going back to work until Sprigs had been properly dealt with. They'd have to consider protective custody for her and Mason at that point.

Melanie turned her back to him and he assumed she was wiping away tears. She kissed the top of Mason's head. A few seconds later, she turned to face him again. "Speaking of touching base with people, I should call my sister. She'll worry if she doesn't hear from me and I can't have her showing up here unannounced."

"My folks will start worrying soon, too. I've been holding off contacting everyone back home until we're all clear. Not sure if Sprigs knows about Mason and I don't want to give him information he doesn't already have. I figure news will spread quickly that I'm a father." Dawson didn't say how easy it would be for Sprigs to make Mason disappear into his network, and that might be the ultimate punishment to Melanie if he couldn't have her.

Dawson also couldn't help noticing how uncomfortable Melanie was every time he mentioned his family.

THE DRIVE TO the lake house ate up most of the morning. The driver of the van had been pleasant and had put on a movie for Mason to keep him occupied. An unmarked sedan drove closely behind them.

Melanie was still shaken by the events of last night.

Now that Sprigs had shown himself, the feds had a starting point to narrow their search. She would hold on to that thought tightly.

Also, the fact that they would be watching her and Mason twenty-four hours a day was a welcome addition. She had Dawson and several law enforcement agencies backing him up. The only daunting thought was how easily Sprigs seemed to get away and how determined he was to take her with him.

A determined psychopath intent on possessing her was the most frightening scenario she could imagine.

Dawson had been quiet on the long ride to the lake house. Based on his intense expression, there had to be a thousand thoughts like hers rolling around in his head.

She had never been to his family's lake house before and she couldn't remember a time when anyone else had, either. Had the family stopped using the place after Bethany died?

The van parked on the pad behind the house.

Two men wearing camo pants, work boots and T-shirts exited the building. They signaled the driver, which must've been the okay sign because he cut off the engine and unlocked the doors.

Dawson stepped outside first. He helped Melanie out after she unbuckled Mason and pulled him to her chest, wincing as he brushed against her burns.

Luckily, he seemed unfazed by the changes in routine.

Melanie had no idea what to expect once she got inside the log cabin. All she really cared about was a soft bed, good security and a workable kitchen in order to prepare meals for Mason.

"Is there any chance there's a crib in there anywhere?" she asked. If not, she could prop pillows around him.

Dawson nodded, pausing for a second before he opened the door and walked in.

The warm-wood, cozy-cabin feeling extended inside. The great room was anchored by a two-story tumbled-stone fireplace. The windows displayed the lake beyond. She'd half expected there to be dust everywhere, but the place had been perfectly preserved.

The great room was open to the kitchen, which had all the necessary appliances. Everything was in good shape and looked barely used. The white appliances were a nice contrast to the darker tile countertops. There was a microwave and a fridge.

"When was the last time you came here?" she asked, looking around. Dawson was right about one thing. No one would expect them to be there.

He didn't answer.

In one corner of the room was a toy box filled with baby dolls, books and Barbie dolls. There was a pink blanket folded neatly on the tan sectional. A thick cotton blanket was folded over the back of part of the sofa.

Melanie looked at Dawson. He stood there, staring out the window toward the lake, looking lost and alone. Based on the intensity of his expression, facing the place was harder than he wanted to acknowledge. And her heart felt as if it were locked in a vise while witnessing his pain. Breathing hurt.

Mason wiggled in her arms, his gaze locked on to the toys.

"Would you like to take him while I get the rest of his

stuff from the van?" she asked Dawson, hoping that holding his son would help ease his pain.

Having Mason was the most grounding experience of Melanie's life. No matter how deep her pain had been at leaving Dawson behind, she'd held tightly to her little boy.

He turned to look at his son, and the pain in his expression only increased.

Her stress that Dawson's mother had been right sat heavy on her chest. Seeing him like this made her fear the worst. If Dawson had known about Mason, it would have ruined his life. And it was too late to turn back now.

"I'll get the stuff from the van," he said, and his voice was gruff.

Was reality hitting him that Mason might've inherited the gene?

Melanie stared out the window, looking at the view. It was another warm sunshiny day in Central Texas. The waves on the lake sparkled like glass.

The heat would be unbearable soon and she'd never felt more hemmed in than she did right now.

She needed air.

Chapter Thirteen

"Want to go outside and see the water, Mason?" Melanie opened the sliding glass door onto the deck facing the water. The temperature felt much cooler on this side of the house and she figured that was most likely because of the breeze off the lake.

Mason's face broke into a wide smile.

"Ma'am," came from behind her.

The voice startled Melanie. She spun around to find one of the agents in camo pants filling the door frame.

"I'd feel more comfortable if you came inside or allowed an agent to accompany you when you leave the house." He introduced himself as Special Agent Norse but asked her to call him Andy.

The whole moment was awkward and uncomfortable, but if it would keep Mason safe, she wouldn't resist. Going inside, seeing Dawson in his current state, would just break her heart all over again. Besides, she knew him well enough to know that he needed time to sort out his feelings. He wouldn't want Mason to see his father struggling to this degree, and Melanie had no idea how to help. The one thing that always worked for her when life overwhelmed her—focusing on Mason—seemed to make the problem worse for Dawson. After all, it was Mason he was concerned about in the first place.

"I'd like to take my son for a walk," she said.

"Mind if I come with you?" Andy was beside them in a heartbeat.

"Sure." She didn't say what she was really thinking… that she wanted to be alone with her son. Besides, Andy was a nice guy and he was only doing his job.

Melanie set Mason down and took his hand. It would do him good to get some exercise after sitting in the van all morning and he seemed eager to explore the new place.

His smile, which was exactly his father's, had a way of brightening even the darkest situations. And it was that smile that she'd focused on when she'd driven her car into a brick wall last night.

"How old is your son?" Andy asked as they cleared the yard and headed toward a path around the lake.

"He's eighteen months." She owed her life to the person who'd invented air bags.

"Got a newborn at home," Andy said.

"Boy or girl?" She smiled. It was nice to talk about something normal for a change.

"Boy. Can't wait until he can start walking. I tease my wife all the time that he's all hers for now. Once he's old enough, we're heading out camping." Andy wore a proud papa smile and it softened his serious expression. He looked like the camping-outside type. He was tan, despite having light hair and blue eyes, and had to be in his early thirties. He was half a foot shorter than Dawson and was built on a sturdy, muscular frame. As nice as he seemed, she had no doubt he'd be deadly. The gun on his hip reminded her of the fact.

"Sounds like fun." She imagined Dawson doing those things with Mason and it made her happy. No doubt having a man in his life would be a great thing for her son. She could see that so clearly now. *If* Dawson could get past his fears. There had been no doubt that he would earlier. That was before she'd seen his expression inside the lake house with all the reminders of Bethany around.

One thing was clear. He was battling demons, and she hoped that he would win for Mason's sake.

And maybe, just a little bit, for her sake, too.

Andy sent a text. "Need to stay in communication with the guys at base so no one gets their feathers ruffled that we're not at the house."

Mason pointed somewhere toward the middle of the lake and started babbling excitedly.

Something out there had him fired up.

How sad was it that Melanie's first reaction was panic?

"Fish," Mason said clearly.

It was the first time he'd used that word. She bent down to his level to see what he was talking about. It seemed Mason was learning a new word every day. He was growing and changing so quickly that she almost wished she could freeze time.

"Mama, fish," he said proudly.

Sure enough, there was a splash twenty-five feet away from them.

"Did that fish jump, Mason?"

He smiled up at her and her heart melted a little more.

"That's a great fish." Andy bent down on the other side of Mason.

Mason clapped his hands. "Fish."

"Stay down," Andy said quietly as he scanned the lake, no doubt making sure there was nothing but fish around. He studied movement on the other side in the swaying grass.

Melanie's heart pounded against her ribs.

A few seconds later, another small splash came.

"All clear," Andy said.

Mason repeated the last word, which came out more like "kere."

Standing on weak legs, she took a deep breath. Everything inside her wanted to go back to the house, close the blinds and hide. The thought Sprigs could be out there somewhere, watching, sent creepy shivers racing up and down her spine.

But could he?

After that crash, he had to be hurt at the very least. No one had actually seen him since, which could mean that he's dead. Couldn't it?

Worrying about her own safety was one thing, thinking about Sprigs hurting Mason…an explosion of anger blasted her in the chest.

She couldn't even go there.

Andy's phone rang. At least they had cell coverage.

Melanie took Mason to the water's edge to get a closer look, gripping his hand tightly. Her all-too-brave little boy would jump in blindly if she let him. To have that kind of trust again. What was that like?

Speaking of which, she needed to call Abby. Her baby sister would be worried that Melanie hadn't reached out. They normally spoke every few days. Abby's classes at University of Texas at Austin would begin soon and she was most likely sucking up the last few days of sunshine at Zilker Park before another crazy-busy semester began and she stayed glued to her laptop or a book.

Melanie wished she'd brought her phone outside with her. She had a no-cell policy when it came to spending time with Mason, and habit had her leaving hers in her purse.

Andy ended his call.

"Special Agent Randall has arrived and would like to speak to you," he said.

Melanie nodded, and then focused on Mason. "Ready to race back to the house, buddy?"

"Uh-huh." Another smile spread across Mason's face revealing tiny white teeth. He turned, let go of Melanie's hand, and burst toward the path.

"Nice. I'll have to remember that one for later," Andy said with appreciation in his voice.

"I learned by watching other moms at the playground. This little trick saves me from many a meltdown." Melanie jogged past the agent, who immediately fell in step behind.

Inside, Melanie scooped up Mason, balanced him on her hip and then scanned the room for Dawson.

There was no sign of him anywhere and that didn't sit well.

A man who was medium height and build with a serious face, wearing dark slacks, a button-down shirt and brown rubber-soled shoes, walked in the back door. He introduced himself as Special Agent Randall.

She crossed the room, exchanged greetings and shook his outstretched hand.

Mason mimicked the gesture, sticking his hand out.

Randall shook Mason's hand next.

"Nice to meet you, big fella," he said, smiling down at her little boy.

Mason smiled shyly.

It was past her son's lunchtime and Melanie figured he'd be getting fussy soon if she didn't get something in his tummy.

"Can we talk in the kitchen?" she asked. "He hasn't eaten yet."

"Take your time," Special Agent Randall said. "I need to update the others anyway. We'll be by the vehicles when you're done."

"Good luck with your little boy," she said to Andy as he filed out of the room.

"Thanks. You have a sweet kid there." He motioned toward Mason.

Dawson walked into the great room, his gaze moving from Andy to Mason with a frown.

"I'll feed him," he said, and his voice was raspy.

One look at his heavy expression and she could see the anguish and sadness written all over his face. It was the same look she'd witnessed all those years ago at his sister's funeral. And the real reason she'd sat on his steps every day afterward until he came out into the sunlight again.

"Can I hold him?" Dawson asked.

"Of course," she said. Mason was already holding his hands out toward his father.

Dawson took him and held him to his chest for a long moment before kissing him on top of his head and releasing a breath.

Melanie, tears soaking her eyes, busied herself pulling together lunch from the food Dawson had packed.

They'd have to go out for more supplies later, but there was enough to get through the afternoon.

After lunch, she cleaned up while Dawson handled the nap routine.

Bethany's crib was still in the master and that was where Dawson told Melanie she should sleep, since it was already set up.

She didn't argue, not in his current state. But they were going to have a conversation about the arrangements later. No way did she feel comfortable sleeping in his mother's bed. Just the thought of that woman sent angry pins poking through Melanie's skin. A rash would've felt better.

Now wasn't the time to get into it.

By the time Dawson came back, Special Agent Randall had returned and Melanie had poured three cups of coffee.

The trio assembled at the massive knotty pine dining table off the kitchen. She had so many questions reeling around in her mind. The dots she was having the most trouble connecting had to do with how any of this was tied to the original abductions.

"Going all the way back to the beginning, how does any of this tie into Thomas Kramer?" Melanie asked. "He took seven-year-old boys. How is he linked to the ring?"

"He was and that's really what led investigators to the operation in the first place. He'd been identifying younger kids, circling back to help abduct them in some cases. He was one of several spotters the masterminds used to target victims. You already know that he worked in the breakdown crew for the Renaissance Festival."

"Why didn't law enforcement figure him out then?" she asked.

"If he was the only one involved, it would've been easier. The trail of kids would have followed the festival and the pattern. They didn't. Most of the kids were much younger and the spotters waited six months or more after the festival had gone to strike. Another problem was that there were other spotters involved and they typically took younger kids."

"Beckett Alcorn has been protected by his father and his money. That couldn't have made it easy to identify him," Dawson added.

"Which is true. Beckett had his father, and his father had a relationship with both the mayor and the sheriff. It was difficult to make the linkages we needed early on," Randall said. "Kramer abducting those seven-year-old boys fourteen years apart had to do with a personal issue. He became greedy."

"What does that mean?" Melanie asked.

"He had a son who died at the age of seven," Randall supplied.

"So Kramer is out there identifying targets and in some cases abducting young kids and he thinks why not take an older one for myself?" Dawson confirmed. "How any father could do that to another parent is beyond me."

"Which is the reason Shane Hughes was located safely earlier this summer," Randall said.

"And what happened to him?" Melanie asked. "What did Kramer do while he had Shane?"

"Not much. He used his aunt Sally to help raise Shane, and by all accounts, he was well cared for. Of course, Kramer lied to her about how Shane came into his life and she didn't question him," Randall said.

"The other boy they found recently. What was his name?" Melanie looked to Dawson.

"Jason," he said.

"What about him? Didn't they find him living in terrible conditions?" Melanie asked.

"Kramer was aging and starting to lose grip on reality before the car crash that killed him. He was hoarding and he kept the boy at that filthy house with him after he lost his job," Randall said. "The best we can tell he must've been trying to figure out another excuse to give his aunt for bringing home another boy not so long after Shane went into the military."

"It's a miracle that Shane's okay. That he was never hurt," Melanie said, tears welling in her eyes. She couldn't even think about Mason being taken away from her and not finding him again until he was grown. She'd always understood her friend Rebecca's need to search for her brother Shane, on some level, especially because Melanie had a little sister that she loved. Now that Melanie was a mother, she couldn't fathom living through the kind of pain Mrs. Hughes had endured or imagine a life without Mason.

She prayed she'd never have to try.

"DID YOU GET anything else out of Beckett this morning?" Dawson asked Randall.

"He's holding strong to his story that Sprigs is the leader and that it's only the two of them in the operation." Randall shook his head. "We know that for the line of bull it is. The problem is that he's lawyered up. Dad is sparing no expense for his son's defense."

"There's no way they could get away with this for so long if it was just the two of them," Dawson agreed.

"Their networks are too sophisticated. They could be aligned with any number of criminal organizations running other 'products' through the state," Randall said. "We've had our eye on a number of possible links."

"I realize that Melanie was just attacked last night, but I'm guessing that this level of security means you think he's going to strike again soon." Dawson glanced at Melanie, whose face had gone pale.

Randall shook his head. "He might be dead and we're hoping to find his body. However, he's escalating his fixation on Ms. Dixon and we believe it's because of the pressure on him."

"Meaning, he's desperate because he fears he'll be caught soon," Dawson clarified.

"That's exactly right. Common sense says he'd lie low for a while. Get out of the country until things cool down here in the States. But this guy is a psychopath. His name is out in the press because of his partner. He knows he can't truly escape. If he shows up at the airport, security will be all over him. Border guards have his picture posted on their walls by now," Randall said.

"Shouldn't that mean he wouldn't be stupid enough to risk coming after me?" she asked.

"He has to know that it's only a matter of time before he's in custody," Randall further clarified. "With time being his enemy, he'll want to strike now if he's alive. Besides, ever since news broke about him, he knows you'll be on guard."

Didn't that send a fireball of anger shooting through Dawson?

"And he already got to me once," she said in a low voice. Her cup suddenly became very interesting to her.

"We're going to do everything we can to ensure that that doesn't happen again, Ms. Dixon," Randall said.

"Thank you," she replied, but there wasn't a lot of feeling behind the words. From the looks of it, Melanie had gone numb.

"I'll use all my resources to protect you," Randall said.

"If he's coming after me, maybe you should disappear with Mason for a while." She looked up, staring into Dawson's eyes.

He'd started shaking his head as soon as he realized where she was going with this.

"It's something to consider," Randall added.

"No can do. It's safer for everyone involved if we stay together." There was no way Dawson was leaving Melanie alone to deal with this jerk. They had protection and there was no reason to believe anyone would be safer by splitting up. "I'm not going anywhere without you, and Mason will be better off here with us."

There was a good reason wars were won by the simple philosophy of divide and conquer. It worked.

Chapter Fourteen

After Special Agent Randall had excused himself, Dawson urged Melanie to lie down. She'd refused to go upstairs, saying she could rest on the couch, but Dawson had insisted. She'd agreed to sleep in the room opposite where Mason was sleeping.

Dawson had been preoccupied, stewing ever since they'd arrived at the lake house, and he was tired of wallowing in his own anger about the past.

Walking through the door of the lake house had been like stepping into quicksand. Dawson had been caught off balance by the emotions that had begun to swallow him. And, similarly, the more he fought the deeper he sank into the pit, and the more he felt he couldn't breathe. He was sinking fast and his resistance was pushing him down faster. He could feel the pressure of something like a wall of wet sand pressing against his chest in a matter of minutes, and he knew he wouldn't survive if he didn't get out of there or get help.

And yet he felt as though he was alone.

Bethany was everywhere in the lake house. Her dolls. Her books. Her favorite blanket. This was the place she'd kept all her real treasures—the place he remembered taking her out to play on the back lawn while she could still walk and romp across the yellow-green grass.

There were countless times she and Dawson had played hide-and-seek or keep-off-the-floor inside the great room, climbing onto the coffee table and hopping onto the couch.

And when her strength was being drained from her little body, when she became frail and could no longer walk or hop on her own, Dawson had helped her onto his back for a piggyback ride just to hear her laugh again. Bethany's laugh was like a spring flower bursting through the cold. Like the sun, it breathed life into all living things. Flowers were brighter. The grass was greener. And life was good.

Maybe it was because her life was cut too short that she was given the kind of smile that could light up even the darkest cave and, later, the darkest day. No way could Dawson hold on to a bad mood when he was around her, no matter how much trouble he'd gotten into with his friends or how long he'd be grounded.

And Bethany's thought that Dawson simply hung the moon was evident in the way she looked up to him.

Their mother had always said how unfair it was that Dawson could draw a full-body laugh from Bethany with a glance in her direction, whereas she had had to work for it.

Saying the two had shared a special bond was a lot like saying ice cream tasted good.

In losing her, Dawson had lost so much more than a little buddy. He'd lost a piece of his soul to a dark place. And he didn't figure he'd get it back again. His heart had fractured, the pieces scattered. There were too many splinters to clean up.

Mason stirred upstairs.

Melanie was still asleep and Dawson didn't want to disturb her. He took the stairs two at a clip, shaking off his sadness, and got to his son before the toddler could wind up a good cry.

But Mason wasn't crying. He was sitting up, looking around the room with his fist half in his mouth.

As soon as he made eye contact, Mason smiled up at Dawson and a feeling, like a burst of joy exploding in his chest, enveloped him.

Looking into his son's eyes was the first time Dawson thought he might begin to pick up the pieces.

"Want to go outside, buddy?" There were a few places he wanted to show Mason after giving him a cup of juice and changing his diaper.

Mason squealed and clapped.

Dawson took care of business first, then grabbed raisins and a juice box before taking Mason by the hand.

The sunshine warmed his face as soon as he stepped outside. Were it not for the breeze coming off the lake, it might be too hot for Mason.

One of the FBI officers followed, hanging back at least twenty feet in order to give them a sense of privacy. Again, Dawson wouldn't argue the intrusion.

There was something he wanted to show his son, if it was still there. Dawson hadn't been out to the lake house in seventeen years.

"Bug!" Mason exclaimed, stopping abruptly and dropping to his knees.

Dawson followed suit.

"That's a roly-poly." He let the little bug crawl onto his finger in order to give Mason a better view.

Mason tried to repeat the words, but they jumbled in his mouth and it was about the darn cutest thing Dawson had ever heard.

After a few seconds of intense study, Mason popped up to standing position and took off running.

Dawson let the bug slide off his finger and followed after the tyke, remembering what Dylan had said when his daughter had come to live with him. Little kids had two speeds…mach and drop dead.

There wasn't much in between in Dawson's observation.

Mason ran toward the hill that Dawson had wanted to show him. On the other side, there was a makeshift fort.

The little boy stopped at the top of the hill. "Water."

Dawson also noted that every word came out excited when Mason was happy. When he was sad, it sounded like the end of the world. Talk about wringing out his heart.

Thankfully, the little guy was rested, fed and happy.

"When you get a little bigger, we can take a boat out there and go fishing," Dawson said.

"Fish?" Mason looked up at him, so serious.

"That's right, buddy. Fish."

Mason clapped and then took off down the hill, his laugh trailed behind him, carried by the breeze.

That must've been a hit. Dawson couldn't wait to take his little guy fishing. Maybe he could talk to his folks about buying the lake house from them, since they never used it anymore, and he and Mason could spend summers there. It was time to build some new memories in this forgotten place.

"Whoa. Slow down, buddy," Dawson said as Mason neared the water's edge. Based on his all-or-nothing attitude, Dawson figured the little tyke would end up running into the water before he realized he'd left grass. This end of the lake was deep.

Mason turned around and a squeal leaped from his mouth as he must've caught sight of the fort.

The side of the hill had been dug out and Dawson had enlisted his father's help to put a wood frame around it.

He'd boarded up the makeshift cave, leaving just enough room for him and Bethany to climb in between the slats. Of course, Dawson was too big to fit inside now, so he pulled out his phone and turned on the flashlight app to allow Mason a peek inside. The elements hadn't affected the place too much. Years of dirt covered the little bench Dawson had dragged inside before boarding it.

It wouldn't take much to clean it up and get it ready.

Mason immediately started climbing through the woods slats, but Dawson stopped him midclimb.

"Hold on there, buddy. You can't go inside the fort without me."

"Fort," Mason said, peeking through the wood, holding on for dear life.

"Yep. That's all yours now," Dawson said, clearing the frog in his throat.

"Mine?" Mason asked.

"Sure is."

"My fort?" Mason asked.

"That's right."

Mason clawed at the boards trying to get inside.

"Dada has to clean it up for you first, big guy," Dawson said.

"Dada?" Mason froze.

For a split second, Dawson wasn't sure if Mason was about to squeal or cry. He hoped he hadn't freaked the little guy out by saying the word too soon. It had sort of slipped out without Dawson thinking about it.

Mason spun around and Dawson put the little tyke's feet on the ground. He didn't hesitate. He barreled into Dawson's knees, repeating the word over and over again. "Dada. Dada. Dada."

His son calling him "Dada" was about the sweetest sound Dawson had ever heard.

"Let Dada show you something else, okay, buddy?"

Mason threw his arms up. Dawson immediately scooped the little guy off his feet, much to Mason's amusement. There was still a lot to learn about caring for a toddler, but Dawson felt good about his progress so far.

His heart melted a little more when Mason threw his arms around Dawson's neck and gave him the best hug of his life. A little more sunlight peeked through the dark caverns in Dawson's heart. This time, Dawson didn't fight it.

Next, he took his son to his favorite place of all time, save for being on the lake itself...the tree house. The tree house was located near the edge of the five-acre property deep into the woods. Instead of inside one tree, it was built using three trees to secure the base. Dawson and his father had located the strongest trees with deep roots and a sturdy trunk.

Using studs in the ground next to the trees minimized the damage to them. The platform came next, all within arm's reach, and then half walls followed by the safety railing.

They'd built it that way specifically for Bethany so she could use it right up until the end. The base of the tree house was four feet off the ground, safe for Mason, and Dawson could easily grab his son if he fell. He and his father had installed a safety rail for Bethany and that would work perfectly for Mason now.

"What do you think, buddy?" Dawson asked as he pointed at it through the trees.

Mason's face lit up.

"It's a tree house," Dawson supplied.

"Twee-house?" Mason questioned. He repeated the new words enthusiastically.

"That's right. You want to go inside?" Dawson asked.

It had been purposely built on a small, sturdy platform for Bethany when she had been sick. It was her favorite place.

The handmade keep-out sign she'd posted over the door still hung proudly. It had been her contribution.

Dawson choked back the emotion threatening to overwhelm him. It somehow seemed right for Mason to be there, running around on the place that had given Bethany so much happiness. The place that she'd asked to be taken to when she spoke her very last words.

If Dawson had known she would never speak again, he would've told her he loved her one more time. Instead, he'd carried her to her favorite rocking chair on the deck facing the lake and held her hand as the sun went down.

He'd fallen asleep next to her, her small bony fingers clamped around his hand, and was woken by the sounds of his mother wailing.

"Dada?" Mason slapped his hands on the railing in excitement, drawing Dawson back to the present.

"Yeah, buddy." He wiped his eyes with the backs of his hands.

"My twee-house?"

"It sure is." Bethany would have loved Mason. And Dawson knew in his heart that she would want to share her favorite place with her nephew.

MELANIE WOKE WITH a start. Something was going on with Mason. She sat up and strained to listen more carefully.

And heard…

Laughter?

Yep, it sure was. Melanie threw the covers off, hopped to her feet and then pulled her hair into a ponytail. By the time she reached the bottom of the stairs, she saw the funniest sight.

Mason and Dawson were sprawled out on the floor,

arms and legs twisted and tangled in an old-fashioned game of Twister.

How many hours had she spent playing that game with her sister when they were bored in the summer? Countless.

"Is this game closed or can I get in on it?" she asked before she thought about how close she'd have to get to Dawson to play. A shiver skittered across her nerves when she thought about skin-to-skin contact.

Dawson was wearing his usual summer wear, athletic shorts and a T-shirt. She tried not to think about the fact that she had on shorts and a halter top. He looked up, winked and fired off a smile. She couldn't pinpoint what it was, but there was definitely something different about him. A good something.

"Mama!" Mason squealed, breaking form and running toward her.

"I guess this game's over. We can start a new one," Dawson offered, and she could tell he was just being nice.

"That's okay. I don't want to ruin your fun," she said. "How long have you two been at this?"

Dawson glanced at the clock over the mantel. "A long time."

Did he feel the same sexual spark that she did every time they were in the same room? She'd thought about the kisses they'd shared one too many nights when she couldn't sleep. "I need to call my sister anyway. I haven't spoken to her in more than a week."

Melanie kissed the top of Mason's head and set him down. He immediately took off toward Dawson.

"Dada," he said, and her heart skipped a few beats. Did he…just…say… *Dada*?

When he repeated the word, she had no doubt she'd heard right the first time. This was coming eventually.

She had to have known that on some level. So why did it catch her off guard?

Maybe because of their extreme circumstances, everything was moving way faster than she ever imagined it would.

Wasn't that a good thing?

Based on the smile on Dawson's face, it was. She'd never seen Mason look happier, too. And she'd be lying if she didn't admit that seeing the two of them together melted her heart.

Melanie located her phone and called Abby.

Voice mail. Great. Melanie waited for the beep and then said, "Hey, little sister, give me a call when you get this message. Love you."

Melanie was hoping to talk to Abby and bring her up to speed.

"She's not picking up?" Dawson asked, his forehead creased with concern.

"No. I'm sure she's at some place like Zilker Park, taking in those last lazy days before her semester starts and life gets out of control," she said. "She started seeing a new guy and she seems really excited about the relationship. I'll call her again in a little while."

Dawson nodded, his attention diverted to Mason, who was about to pull a box of checkers off the shelf and onto his head.

"Better leave that to me," Dawson said, rescuing Mason just before the dump.

"Mama. My twee-house," Mason said, pointing to a picture.

Melanie tossed a confused look toward Dawson before moving to her son's side. The picture was of a healthy Bethany, who was all smiles, sitting at the entrance to a tree house. "That's wonderful, Mason."

"My twee-house," Mason said with an earnest expression. "Mine."

Melanie chanced a glance at Dawson, careful not to intrude on what could be a difficult moment.

"It's okay," Dawson reassured her, and he looked so much better than when they'd first arrived at the lake house hours ago. "I took him there to show it to him while you were sleeping. I think it's safe to say that it belongs to him now."

Behind his smile a deeper emotion was brewing. Melanie decided not to push her luck.

"Are you hungry?" she asked Mason, turning away from the beautiful little girl's picture. It was hard for Melanie to look, to be reminded of Bethany and the disease that took her life so young.

Melanie hugged Mason a little tighter.

He wiggled out of the hug.

"Mine."

"I know, sweetheart," Melanie said with a smile, letting him stare at the picture.

Maybe she should've scheduled an appointment with a genetic specialist. It wouldn't hurt to find out if Mason carried the gene. But then what would happen? She'd had this argument in her head a thousand times and there was never a good answer. None of it would change the way she loved him or the fact that she wanted him to have a normal childhood for as long as possible. Knowing would just color every day with a dark cloud.

"I've got this. Why don't you take a break?" Dawson asked. It was more statement than question. He left to put Mason down to sleep after dinner and their nighttime routine.

Melanie agreed. If he'd taken their son to the places he'd shared with his sister, then he probably needed Mason more than she did. Dawson had slipped into a comfortable routine with their son, looking so much more at ease than he had in those first few days.

Nothing like a crash course in child care to get a person up to speed, Melanie thought. She'd had the same one when the little guy was born. Or maybe it just came naturally for parents to care for their child. Natural? Melanie choked back a laugh as she put away the last of the dishes. Not exactly the word she would've used to describe those first few weeks at home with Mason after her mother left.

Then again, he was a lot tinier back then. So much more fragile.

She walked past the bottle of wine and made coffee instead. She poured two cups.

Dawson, none the worse for wear, appeared just in time to enjoy a fresh mug.

"Care for one?" she asked.

"Do I?" Dawson picked up his and shot her a sideways glance when he picked up hers, too, and then balanced them while he opened the sliding glass door. "Coming?"

"What about Mason?"

"I'll leave the door open so we can hear him if he wakes. He was pretty tired when I put him to bed, though." He nodded toward the deck. "C'mon."

"Okay." Melanie followed him outside, where he pulled two Adirondack chairs and a side table in front of the door. He closed the screen door behind them to keep out bugs.

"I see you're taking up my bad habit," he said, and she knew he was referring to coffee instead of Pepsi. She'd already had two of those.

"It's not so bad."

"How's this?" he asked, hesitating when his gaze landed on a small white rocking chair.

It was the perfect size for a five-year-old. That had to have been hers.

Melanie's heart squeezed. She touched his arm, ignoring the charge of electricity shooting through her hand and spiking her blood pressure.

"You want to go back inside?" she asked.

"No. I don't." He stared at it for a long moment and then took his seat, focusing on the lake instead. "I want to be right here. With you."

Those last two words didn't help at all with the blood pulsing through her veins or just how aware her body was of him when he was this close. She needed to redirect her energy. "I'm pretty sure you made Mason's day today. He loves it out here."

"I see some of Bethany in him," Dawson said almost so quietly that she didn't hear him.

Melanie took a sip of coffee. She'd seen it, too. She chose to think of it as Dawson.

"Are you against having him tested?" Dawson asked. He took another sip of coffee and stared at the sky.

"I just haven't, I guess."

"Well, have you spoken to your pediatrician about the possibility?" Dawson pressed.

If there was a right answer to this, Melanie sure didn't know what it was. Just talking about it with Dawson had her hands sweaty and mouth dry. She took another sip of coffee to relieve the itch in her throat.

"Believe it or not, I'm not trying to be a bastard by asking," he said.

"I didn't say you were," she snapped back too quickly. Did this topic make her uncomfortable? Yes. It did. Did that make her an awful mother? Dawson could judge her all he wanted to. She hadn't brought it up and hadn't had him tested. There. Sue her.

"You don't have to be defensive. I know we got off on a bad start, but in case you hadn't noticed I've been trying to work with you," he said, and his tone was indignant. "It's not an unrealistic conversation to have, Melanie. I need to know."

"Would it matter? Would you love him less?" She hated how shaky her voice had become.

"That's not fair." No matter how calm his voice was, her pulse was still rising.

"Neither is knowing your son could die." She pushed off the chair and stalked to the edge of the deck, stopping to grip the rail. She'd known that it would only be a matter of time before they would have this conversation, and yet she hadn't expected it to come this fast or hurt this much. "And it wouldn't change my love for Mason. I want him to have a normal life no matter what."

Dawson didn't respond, and she half feared the storm that was brewing.

Instead of yelling as she'd half expected, he was suddenly behind her and his arms encircled her waist.

"It's me, Melanie. You don't have to be angry with me." His deep timbre ran along the base of her neck, down her spine.

"I'm not," she lied. It was partly true.

"No. You're scared." His voice wrapped around her.

Despite wanting to fight it, to fight him, to fight the world, her body relaxed against his muscled chest. Because it was Dawson. And she felt safe in his arms.

"And I'm scared, too." His voice came out as a whisper against her neck. "But we can get through this together."

Then he kissed her. His lips so soft against the skin of her neck.

Heat swirled through her body.

She unclasped his hands, kissed each of them and then

let them go. Instead of falling at his sides, they landed on the guardrail, and on either side of her, pinning her.

She shouldn't allow this to go any further, and she knew that somewhere in the back of her mind. She was reaching the point of no return, and if he didn't stop she wouldn't be able to.

Melanie turned around. Her hip firmly planted against the rail. He leaned forward, resting his forehead against hers. And she could tell the instant her body changed from anger to awareness…awareness of Dawson's strength… awareness of his masculinity…awareness of the strong man standing in front of her.

So she didn't fight, couldn't fight when his lips crushed down on her, hungry. He groaned against her mouth. There wasn't much more that she could do except surrender to the heat, to the scorching flames engulfing her. Every part of her body came alive, sensitized, as she parted her lips for him and drove her tongue inside his mouth.

The cool breeze danced across her hot skin.

A thought struck. There were FBI agents watching the lake house.

It must've occurred to Dawson about the same time because he pulled back and then glanced around.

"You want to take this inside?" he asked, his gaze piercing through all her carefully constructed walls, shattering all her intellectual reasons why this shouldn't happen. This all came down to being a man and a woman, basic desire, and there was no man she wanted more than Dawson.

"Yes."

"Just so there's no misunderstanding. You realize what I'm asking," he said, and his voice was deep and gravelly.

"I already gave you my answer," she said. "Unless you think we shouldn't."

He twined their fingers and walked inside, closing and locking the sliding door behind them.

Flipping off lights as they moved through each room, she figured he was stalling, giving her time to change her mind. Did he want her to be the sensible one?

When they made it to the bottom of the steps, she tugged his hand. He turned around and she let go of his hand, wrapping her arms around his neck instead. She had to push up to her tiptoes to kiss him, but she did, pressing her body flush with his.

There was no mistaking that he wanted this as badly as she did when his erection pressed to her belly. That fired molten lava through her veins, melting any protests she might have had before they could take seed.

Yes, on an intellectual level having sex with Dawson would be a bad idea. It would complicate their situation even more if that was possible.

Physically, though, and from a place buried deep in her heart, those arguments didn't hold water. Being with Dawson made perfect sense and felt so incredibly right.

With his arms around her waist, he claimed her mouth again, deepening the kiss when she moaned against his lips. And Melanie melted against him.

He pulled back a little.

"Upstairs," he said, his mouth moving against hers.

"Yes. Now." She stepped around him and headed up first.

After quickly checking on Mason, who was sleeping peacefully in his crib, Melanie followed Dawson to his bedroom.

Her heart pounded, her skin tingled and there was something that felt a lot like ache penetrating her body.

She had never felt so intense, so much chemistry, so much heat—with anyone other than Dawson.

Mostly, because there was so much more between them than physical attraction, even though they had that in spades.

Did he feel the same?

Could she go through with this if he didn't?

"Dawson," she said.

When he turned to look at her, there was so much hunger in his eyes.

"We need to talk," she said.

Chapter Fifteen

"We need to talk?" Dawson echoed. Those four words were normally sex-drive killers. In Melanie's case, he'd make an exception and that was mostly because he had no control over his body's reaction to her. If she wanted to put the brakes on, he'd need one damn cold shower at this point. "Now?"

"I want...*this*." She sat on the edge of the bed. "But I need to know that it won't change things between us."

"In what way?" he asked. "Because I was hoping it would."

"We have a lot going on and I don't want to be walking on eggshells with each other," she said.

"Like we haven't been already?" he asked with a smirk. He had yet to be comfortable around Melanie since seeing her again and finding out they had a child together.

She burst into a smile. And it was about the sexiest thing Dawson had ever seen.

"Yeah, I guess you're right. It has been intense, hasn't it?" she asked.

"I'll understand if you've changed your mind about this." He glanced toward the bed.

Melanie stood and then pulled her shirt over her head. It didn't make a sound when it hit the floor. She stood there in front of him, wearing a lacy black bra. Her chest moved up and down quickly as he remembered the feel of her firm breasts in his hands.

Dawson closed the distance between them in two steps.

"You're beautiful, Melanie." That her cheeks flushed with the compliment stirred his heart. "And damn sexy."

Her gaze locked on to his when she shimmied out of her shorts.

Dawson groaned when he caught a glimpse of her panties. Black. Silky. Lined with lace. Just like her bra.

He ran his finger along the inside edge of her bra in a V. He remembered how sweet she tasted, and the urge to run his tongue along the same spot assaulted him.

"Dawson, I want you. *Now*." The urgency in her words turned him on. She made a move toward the bed, but he stopped her.

"I've thought about this moment for too long to rush." She wasn't making it easy. He tugged her toward him and kissed her, hoping to slow things down a notch.

It didn't help.

If anything, that kiss was like pouring gasoline on a fire. The explosion of need rushed through him just as out-of-control as the blaze.

Desire warred with his self-control, and his self-control was losing the battle.

He pulled back, eyes closed, and tried to think of something else…anything else…something mundane…like changing the oil on his SUV.

"You're not getting away with that, Dawson Hill." Melanie always could tell what he was thinking. "Look at me."

He opened his eyes at the same time her bra hit the floor, along with Dawson's reserves.

He spread his hand across her full breast, and her nipple beaded against his palm. Damn. Sexy.

Her tongue slicked across her bottom lip, leaving a

silky trail, and Dawson was mesmerized—mesmerized by the sweetness of her skin, the hold she had over him and the sense of belonging he felt when he slid inside her. Which, at this rate, wasn't going to be too long.

It only took another two seconds to strip his clothes off. Her panties joined the floor at the same time.

And there she was, his Melanie. Sweetness, intelligence and sex appeal rolled into one helluva blond-haired, brown-eyed package.

Dawson put his arms around her waist and lowered her onto the bed as gently as he could given how much restraint it took not to pick her up and drive himself deep inside her right then and there. Every muscle corded with tension, needing release.

And he'd only just begun.

He pushed himself up on bent knees and slicked his tongue down her chest until her beaded nipple was inside his mouth. Licking and sucking, enjoying every moan he got out of Melanie, Dawson slid his tongue down her belly, pausing long enough to kiss the stretch marks that had been created when she gave him a son.

And then he moved his mouth down, positioning himself in between her thighs.

Melanie tasted sweet, and the fact that she was already wet nearly sent him over the edge. He pushed the thought aside and delved his tongue inside her sweet heat.

"Oh, Dawson." He liked the sound of his name on her tongue.

Deeper. His tongue surged inside her as he used his thumb to draw circles on her mound.

Faster. He felt her body arch and tense and he knew she was nearing release.

"I want you inside me. Now." Melanie scooted toward the foot of the bed and then clasped her legs around Dawson's midsection.

He dipped his tip inside her and nearly lost all control. Her fingers dug into his back and he knew that she was teetering on the edge.

He drove inside her and she matched his stride.

As he thrust deeper, his own need was like a bomb about to detonate despite his best efforts to contain it.

When he could feel her muscles clench around his shaft, he allowed himself to release, falling off the edge with her.

Careful not to crush her with his weight, he eased her toward the pillow, not ready to pull out before it was absolutely necessary. And that was when he realized that they hadn't used protection.

"Melanie." Dawson eased to her side and pulled her against his chest. Their arms were still in a tangle and he could feel her racing heartbeat. "We didn't—"

"I'm on the pill. I won't get pregnant again this time," she reassured.

"Would it be so bad to give Mason a sibling?"

"Funny joke. I think our hands are full as it is, don't you?"

She thought he was kidding? Maybe she couldn't read him anymore. Because he knew in his heart that he meant it.

"I still love you. What more is there?"

Damn. Did he say that out loud?

And there was no reaction from Melanie.

Didn't he know how to quiet a room?

A quick jab to his arm came a second later. Melanie's laugh filled the awkward silence.

"Quit trying to be funny, Dawson."

He went along with the misunderstanding, ignoring the pain in his chest that she didn't believe him.

On second thought, maybe it wasn't the worst thing in the world right now. They were already heavily invested in feelings, they'd just had the best sex he could remember and love complicated their situation even more.

There were a lot of details to work out between them now that they shared a son. And maybe it was better that she didn't know he loved her, because Dawson had a feeling they didn't see eye to eye on a few important matters with regard to Mason. Until they sorted things out, it was best to take things one step at a time.

Besides, Dawson might have to play hardball to bring her to the light. And he would if that was the only choice she gave him.

Melanie softened his thoughts when she curled herself around him and fell into a deep sleep on his chest.

"I love you, Melanie," he whispered as he closed his eyes and then drifted off.

DAWSON MIGHT HAVE been joking last night, but Melanie's heart had stopped when he said he still loved her. Normally, she could read the man's mind, but her own confused feelings got in the way when it came to love, and her heart wished he'd said it for real.

Exactly the reason she needed to slow down and keep a level head.

Melanie untangled herself from Dawson's arms, thinking that was the best she'd slept in...she couldn't remember how long. She slipped out of bed and into the shower before Mason opened his eyes.

Once that whirlwind woke, Melanie had precious little time for herself.

She enjoyed the feel of the warm water. Since Dawson had come into their lives, she'd had several quiet showers.

By the time Mason woke and called for her, she'd dressed and had a few sips of coffee while standing at the sliding door, enjoying the view of the sun rising across the lake. This place was perfectly positioned to take advantage of sunsets, and she could easily see why the family had bought it. And she could also see why they wouldn't come back after they'd lost Bethany. This place had to have been special to her.

Melanie took the stairs, stopping at the top. She thought she'd heard Mason calling for her, but he was saying, "Dada."

And Dawson was a few steps away from his crib.

Her heart melted in her chest at the sight of them. Mason's wide smile. Dawson's outstretched arms.

She didn't want to intrude on the moment, so she tiptoed downstairs and poured a cup of coffee for Dawson.

This was nice. Was it even possible that this could be real? That it could last…no…it was almost too perfect. How long before the tiny cracks would seep through and break the facade?

And how devastating would that be?

With a normal man, Melanie could handle it. Not with Dawson. There was something too special about the bond they'd shared to allow that to happen.

All those negative thoughts shattered when Dawson appeared, shirtless, carrying a smiling Mason against his chest.

"Mama!" Mason exclaimed, happy to see her but not exactly trying to get down so he could run to her.

"Good morning, big boy," she said with a smile.

Dawson kissed her on the cheek and then Mason followed suit.

How adorable was that?

Melanie held out Dawson's cup of coffee when she heard a rustling noise at the door. Her first thought was one of the FBI agents noticed movement in the house and wanted to use the bathroom. But then, they wouldn't have a key, would they?

The back door swung open and, shock of all shocks, Alice Hill walked in behind Andy who wore an apology on his face. Dawson's father, Jack, trailed closely behind.

"The alarm company notified us of activity here at the house, so we decided to come see for ourselves what was going on. This agent interrogated us before allowing us onto our own property," Alice said coolly. Her ice-cold gaze stopped on Melanie, and disapproval was stamped all over her tense features.

"Again, my apologies, ma'am" Andy said to Alice. He looked at Dawson. "You have this under control?"

Dawson nodded before Andy excused himself.

"I didn't realize you'd brought a *friend* out here, Dawson."

Melanie stood there like a concrete statue, frozen in time, and she was sure her jaw had hit the floor. In no way and under no circumstances was she ready to face Dawson's mother.

Unable to breathe with that woman in the room, Melanie grabbed her son and bolted out the slider.

She vaguely heard Dawson calling her name, but she didn't stop until she reached Andy's sedan.

He turned toward her. "Everything okay, Ms. Dixon?"

"Yes. Sure. Will you take me and my son out to get something to eat?" she asked, pleading with her eyes.

Andy opened the back door with a knowing smile.

"You have a car seat already?" she asked.

"Have to be ready to go at a moment's notice," he said.

Right. Of course.

She buckled Mason in, praying that Dawson wouldn't burst out the nearest door.

He didn't, and she figured he was backed against the wall by his parents and trying to explain why the heck she was at their lake house with federal officers and their grandchild.

Melanie didn't need to see Alice's face again to know how much she disapproved of the pregnancy, of Mason. After all, that shocked image had been burned into Melanie's memory nearly two and a half years ago. Her words wound through Melanie's thoughts like weeds choking a flower. She tried to block them out, focusing instead on the gravel road leading away from the lake house.

"Thank you," she said to Andy.

"No problem," he replied before transmitting their change in location. "You looked like you'd seen a ghost."

"I hope I didn't freak you out or anything. It's just, well, that woman really knows how to get under my skin." How crazy was Melanie to think a life with Dawson and their child would work out? Alice was probably back there undermining Melanie before she even got out of earshot.

Then again, once she admitted to knowing about their son and pushing Melanie away, Dawson would have to see his mother for the...bully...she was.

Thinking about family was giving Melanie a headache. It was too early in the morning for this drama. Darn it. Family. Melanie hadn't remembered to bring her phone. She hadn't checked it yet this morning and she didn't know if Abby had called.

She would ask to borrow Andy's cell phone if she'd been smart enough to memorize the number. She hadn't. Everyone was a name in her contact list now. She couldn't remember the last time she'd memorized an actual phone number other than hers.

As soon as she returned to the lake house, she needed to find her phone and check to see if Abby had called.

"Has Sprigs been found yet?" she asked, knowing this operation would most likely be over if he had.

"No. We have people covering your place, though. If he so much as sets foot within a mile, we'll get him," Andy said.

"Is there still a possibility that he might be hurt or hiding?"

"There is." There was no commitment in his words.

And what that really told her was that Sprigs could be anywhere. She tightened her grip on her seat belt and glanced at Mason.

Andy's cell buzzed causing Melanie to jump at the sudden noise.

"Sorry," she said. "Guess I'm on edge."

"It's okay," he said with a smile. "I have a mother-in-law, too."

Melanie stopped herself before she said that she wasn't related to that crazy woman back there in any way, shape or form. She needed to watch herself in front of Mason. Like it or not, Alice was most likely going to be in her son's life, and Mason was a sponge. She didn't want him picking up on her dislike for his grandmother.

Besides, it would be Dawson's responsibility to make sure his parents saw their child. Mason could visit on Dawson's time, and Melanie wouldn't have to be anywhere around the woman who'd made it clear she didn't want to have anything to do with her.

Andy had pulled off to the side of the country road in order to take the call. He gave an apologetic look before holding the phone out to her. "It's for you."

"Why would that be for me?" She stared at the cell as if it were a bomb about to detonate, scooting back toward the door behind her. If she could crawl out the window to get away from that thing, she would.

"It's Mr. Hill. He asked to speak to you." Andy paused when she balked. "You want me to take a message?"

"Would you?" Her eyes pleaded again.

Andy nodded.

"Tell him I'm busy with Mason, but we'll be back soon," she said, realizing Dawson was most likely checking up on her to make sure she didn't disappear on him again. That hurt.

Andy said a few *uh-huh*s and *yes, sir*s into the phone before he ended the call and navigated the sedan onto the winding road.

"Sorry. We had a fight." It wasn't exactly a lie. She was pretty sure they were about to have it out when she got home. Or maybe Dawson would be too upset with his mother to be mad at her.

Alice would most likely spin the whole story to her advantage. And then what would happen after? The pressure to have Mason tested would be enormous. Melanie had planned to discuss the issue with her pediatrician. She'd been waiting…no… Dawson was right last night. She'd been too scared to bring it up.

She'd been ignoring the fact that a remote possibility existed that her son would be anything but perfectly healthy.

The pressure on her chest while thinking about it now was like a bull sitting on her ribs. Her thoughts were heavy and it was like a thick, dark cloud had settled over her brain.

Mason was in the backseat making raspberry sounds.

Seeing him, knowing he was okay calmed her below panic levels.

He was such a happy boy.

And she prayed that he would stay healthy, too.

Chapter Sixteen

Dawson was fuming by the time Melanie returned to the lake house. She could tell based on how red the base of his neck had become. She had to give him credit. He held it all inside as he greeted them.

She'd intentionally stayed away until his parents had gone, lying to herself by saying that she was giving them time to talk. Actually, she was being a coward because she wasn't ready to face Alice just yet. And especially not after what had happened between her and Dawson last night.

Tensions thickened between them while they played with Mason, fed him and then put him down for his afternoon nap.

"Where'd you go this morning?" Dawson demanded. He had every right to be mad. She'd done the same to him when he up and disappeared at her apartment last week.

"To breakfast with Andy."

Dawson's eyes sparked with anger. "Oh, it's Andy now?"

"What?" Was he jealous?

"Never mind. Why did you take off like that with Mason?" Dawson said, moving into the kitchen, and she realized that was the farthest point from Mason's room upstairs.

"Because it was awkward, okay?"

"You can't just run away every time things get tough, Melanie." A muscle in Dawson's neck bulged. Not a good sign. And he'd scored a direct hit with her.

"Hold on a second. I thought you would want time alone with your folks to explain what was going on."

"One look at Mason and they figured it out, Melanie."

She blew out a frustrated breath. Really? Seriously? Had Alice played it as though she didn't know about Mason?

"I'll bet they did," came out on a huff.

"What's your problem?" Dawson said, the muscle throbbing.

She could appreciate that she'd left him in an uncomfortable position to defend himself in front of his parents. And she could further acknowledge that it would be difficult to face Alice alone. The woman had scared Melanie half to death with her threats. But for Dawson to ask Melanie what *her* problem was, well, that was just ridiculous.

"That's not a serious question." She shook her head. "What did your mother say?"

"That she can't wait to get to know her grandchild."

Melanie balked. "I bet."

"What does that mean?" he asked, looking hurt in addition to being angry.

"I don't know what kind of game she's playing, but your mother does not want to spend time with Mason."

"What's your problem with her? What has she ever done to you to make you so bitter?" Dawson asked, incredulous. His mother really knew how to play him, which was odd considering that she hadn't been all that concerned about her son after Bethany died.

Melanie didn't respond. Couldn't respond. Anger filled her as she thought about the things Alice had said to her.

"Every time I bring her up, you have a reaction," he pressed.

"Leave it alone, Dawson."

"What? The fact that you hate my mother? Why should I? She's Mason's grandmother and she's going to be part of his life," Dawson said. "I know she isn't perfect, but she's excited to be a grandmother."

"Oh, that really does it." Melanie fumed. "Excited to be a grandmother?"

"That's the exact word she used."

"I didn't realize there'd be a snowstorm blowing through this morning to blind you, but you need to open your eyes, Dawson."

"To what? The fact that you can't stand my family? How can we have any kind of future together if that's the case?"

"I like your family just fine, Dawson. Or I did. Right up until the time your mother ran a pregnancy test on me when all I thought I had was the flu." She regretted those words as soon as they left her mouth. She hadn't intended to tell Dawson this way. His relationship with his parents had been so broken when Bethany died. They'd managed to repair enough of the damage to have a bond and she shouldn't take that away no matter how frustrated she got or how horrible his mother had behaved.

Dawson whirled around on her so fast she had to take a second to catch her breath. He would never hurt her, she would never have to worry about that, but she'd knifed him in the chest with her betrayal, and the hurt in his eyes nearly brought her to her knees.

"You went behind my back with my family?" he managed through gritted teeth. "What else have you been hiding?"

She deserved that. "Nothing. And I didn't want to tell you like this."

"Then how, Melanie? How did you intend to lie to me and break my heart again? Did you wait until I fell for you again on purpose? So you could rip my heart out and stomp on it? Again?" Dawson's fist pounded the tile countertop.

Tears stung the backs of her eyes as his image blurred in her vision. All she could do was be honest, put her cards on the table and hope that he understood.

"She threatened me. She told me that she'd take my child away if I told you about the pregnancy."

"I don't believe you," he said through clenched teeth.

Melanie kept going. "Said that I would be trapping you into a life of misery, especially if the baby inherited the disease."

"She would never say something like that," he seethed.

"That's the real reason I left Mason Ridge. I didn't want you to hate me and I knew you'd never be able to let it go if Mason inherited the disease, and it would destroy you."

"Even if she said that, and I don't for one minute believe any of it's true, why wouldn't you let me decide for myself?" he asked with hurt all over his tone.

She didn't have a good answer for that except that she remembered what Bethany's sickness and death had done to Dawson and couldn't force him to go through it again with his own child.

"After everything we've been through together, that's how little you thought of me when you knew me better than anyone else in the entire world?" he asked.

"I do know you, Dawson. And your mother said every

last word of what I just told you," she said, defensive. Melanie should've been honest with Dawson, that part was true, but she'd be damned if she'd allow him to go on thinking his mother would never do something like that and this was all her fault.

Dawson looked at her. The hurt in his eyes robbed her breath.

Had she done all this for Dawson? Or had a big part of her been afraid that she'd end up just like her parents…in an empty marriage?

"You're a liar." He walked toward the door without looking back, pausing as he filled the frame. "And if it weren't for Mason, I'd never want to see you again."

He left.

If Melanie could move, she'd drop to her knees. She couldn't. Instead, she stood there rooted to the kitchen floor for what felt like an eternity, stupidly wishing she could take it all back and start the day over. Hell, she wished she could go back and change all her bad decisions.

She couldn't.

If life had taught her one thing, it was that there were no do-overs. People made mistakes. Period. Wallowing in them wouldn't do any good.

Hurting Dawson hadn't been part of her plan. None of this had. She hadn't expected to be scared by his mother and pushed away. She hadn't expected to be stalked by a psychopath. And she sure as hell hadn't expected to reunite with the one man she loved. Loved?

That part was true enough. There was no use denying it. Being in his arms last night was the first time she'd felt truly alive since she disappeared from town.

Melanie could admit now that she'd committed serious errors in judgment. She'd give almost anything to correct them. Dawson would never forgive her. Between his mother and her own messed-up parents, Melanie was beginning to believe she would never be able to open herself up to another person again. How on earth had everything gotten so twisted?

When two hours had passed and he still hadn't returned, she packed up both her and Mason's things.

Andy had to call it in, but he was able to get permission from Randall to take her to another safe house.

Because Melanie couldn't stay in that house any longer. Not with the way her heart felt as if it would explode right out of her chest.

She scribbled a note for Dawson to let him know that she and Mason were moving to a safe house and that she'd be in touch to make visitation arrangements as soon as this ordeal was behind them.

And then she walked out the door.

This time, she looked back and her heart wanted Dawson to be standing there more than she wanted to breathe.

He wasn't.

And she had no idea when he would return.

DAWSON CIRCLED THE lake again, trying to walk off his anger. He'd learned at a young age that anger made everything worse and yet he couldn't stop himself. It was Melanie and he would've thought, would've liked to believe, that she knew him better than that.

He'd come down hard on her. It had only taken forty-six laps for him to calm down enough to realize it.

If what she'd said about his mother was true, and Dawson didn't want to believe it could be, then he owed her an apology.

They had a lot of work to do if they were going to make this...whatever *this* was...work. He thought they'd made strides toward being able to talk about difficult subjects and being able to depend on each other, so he'd overreacted.

If what Melanie said was true, then his mother should be the one to receive his fury. And he had every intention of sitting the woman down and talking to her about why she would pull such a stunt.

So much made sense about Melanie's actions after she'd learned that she was pregnant. And he'd been a first-class idiot with the way he treated her. He could only hope that she'd give him another chance.

As he was walking back toward the lake house, the first thing Dawson noticed was that Andy's sedan wasn't parked out back. Didn't that put a searing-hot branding iron through Dawson's gut?

He reminded himself to calm down even as his instincts had his feet moving faster toward that door.

Dawson broke into a run.

He didn't stop until he was inside the lake house. He called out for Melanie, but the place was quiet—too quiet because Mason should be wide-awake right now and running around. That boy was a flurry of activity, excitement and nonstop energy.

His absence pierced Dawson somewhere deep in his heart with painful stabs of loneliness.

The place felt so empty without Mason, without Melanie.

Dawson searched the upstairs, confirming what he already knew.

There was a note taped to Mason's crib.

I'm truly sorry for all the pain I've caused you, Dawson.

I never intended to hurt you. You're my best

friend and I've missed you beyond belief. You should know up front that I have no intention of keeping your son away from you. He needs you as much as you need him. Seeing the two of you together, the bond you've already formed, makes it that much harder to walk away right now. But until this is over, it's not safe. Mason is not safe.

As soon as Sprigs is caught, we'll be back. I wish I could tell you where we're going. I don't even know. But I'll do anything to keep our son safe until this is over and we can set up a normal routine—whatever "normal" means anymore.

Love,

Melanie

Dawson hadn't cried since Bethany died. Until a tear broke loose and streaked his cheek just now. He choked his emotion back and told himself to take a minute to toughen up.

He fished his cell phone out of his jeans pocket and called Melanie.

She didn't pick up and, on some level, he'd expected that.

His next call was to Randall.

"Where is she?" Dawson didn't bother to hide his anger.

"I can't tell you that, but I can tell you that she and Mason are safe," Randall said, an apology laced his tone.

"Send someone to pick me up," Dawson said. "Take me to them."

"I would if I could," Randall said. "That's not possible right now. I know you would never want me to jeopardize the safety of Ms. Dixon or your son."

Randall had that much right.

But Dawson had every intention of taking matters into his own hands.

Chapter Seventeen

Dawson paced while he waited for his parents to circle back and pick him up. The hour that had passed felt like an eternity, and he wasn't any closer to figuring out where Sprigs might be.

If he had to visit Alcorn in jail to pressure him for information, Dawson would.

There were other pressing questions with people closer to home that were about to give Dawson a headache. He needed to know the truth about what had happened between Melanie and his mother. He couldn't fathom his mother going behind his back, and at the same time he couldn't picture Melanie lying about something this important.

The second he heard gravel crunching underneath tires, he locked the door and met his folks as they pulled onto the parking pad.

"Can you take me to my SUV?" he asked immediately.

"Yes, of course," his mother said as Dawson climbed into the back of her Escalade.

His father was driving and that gave Dawson the perfect opportunity to speak to his mother without either of them being distracted.

"Was Melanie a patient of yours, Mother?" he asked outright as his father reversed out of the driveway.

Mother's jaw went slack, but she quickly recovered.

"I believe she did come see me once or twice." She looked to be digging deeply to recall the information.

There was another explanation that Dawson didn't want to consider. She was stalling.

"Which is it, Mother? Once or twice?" he pressed.

"I'm not sure. It was a while ago and I see a lot of people in town," his mother said.

"How many who come in with the flu do you end up running pregnancy tests on, Mother?"

Her face puckered like a prune as she stared out the front windshield.

Dawson waited for a response.

None came.

"Then let's narrow the field down to women I've dated," he said.

"Son, what exactly are you accusing your mother of?" Dawson's dad, who had been quiet up to now, asked as he spun the wheel, navigating the winding country road.

"Are you saying that you don't know already?" Dawson asked in return.

"I have no idea what you're talking about." Dawson's father paused. "Alice?"

Still nothing from her.

"Then let me tell you," Dawson began.

"Oh, all right," his mother said, cutting him off. "Melanie did come to my office saying she thought she had the flu. I knew right away what the real problem was, so I had the nurse ask for a urine sample."

Problem? Did she just refer to Dawson's son as a problem?

"The test came back positive, so I did what I had to in order to protect you," she continued, her voice so matter-of-fact it sent a chill down Dawson's back.

"You did this for me?" he asked, incredulous. "You threatened the woman carrying my child and kept my son from me for his first year and a half of life, and you have the audacity to say you did it *for me*?"

"Alice," Dawson's father said, sadness and disappointment in his tone.

"What choice did I have?" she defended, folding her arms.

"The best thing you can do for yourself right now is keep your mouth closed, Alice," Dawson's father said. "And pray that your son finds it in his heart to forgive you someday."

"I doubt that will ever happen," Dawson quipped.

"Tell me you don't mean that, son," Dawson's father said. "Your mother has done a terrible thing—"

His mother made a move to interrupt his father.

"Alice. Let me say my piece," he said quickly.

She harrumphed, picking invisible lint off her suit jacket.

"It's unforgivable to think she would do something like this. And I won't lie and say she had your best interest at heart, because I don't believe it, either. What I will say is that she believed she had your best interest at heart because she loves you. And losing Bethany changed all of us. Not all of it was for the better."

No one immediately spoke, and that was most likely because there was a lot of truth to those words.

Alice's chest deflated. "He's right. When he puts it like that, I realize how terribly I've overreacted. I didn't know how to fix it once I'd set things in motion. Then she disappeared and I tried my best to forget what I'd done. For all I knew she wouldn't follow through with the pregnancy, so I left it alone. You might never be able to forgive me, but I didn't lie about one thing, I'm beyond thrilled to have a grandchild. I hope I haven't messed up any chance I had to have a relationship with your son."

Dawson would forgive his mother at some point. And he wouldn't keep Mason from her in order to punish her. Too much time had been lost with the people he loved to allow that to happen. Still, he was going to need some time to absorb this news.

He leaned back against the seat and closed his eyes, wondering if the damage with Melanie was even close to repairable.

"I just want you—"

"Let him be, Alice," Dawson's father said. "Give the man time to think."

He was grateful for the interception. If his mother was genuine, and he believed she was, then he could find a way to forgive her. There were a dozen more pressing thoughts running through his mind right now.

His phone buzzed, indicating he had a text.

Dawson pulled it from his pocket and checked the screen. His heart raced when he saw the name, Melanie.

I can't reach Abby and they won't let me look for her. Said they'd handle it themselves. Please help.

It wasn't the message Dawson was hoping for, but it was a start. He wouldn't refuse her plea.

Can you tell me where you are?

He waited for a response.

No. I'm sorry.

He expected that and he didn't want to push it. He'd had to ask.

We're okay. Mason is asking for you.

Reading that message shattered the darkness inside him and filled Dawson's heart with light.

How about you?

He wanted to know where he stood with her.

She didn't respond, which wasn't necessarily a bad thing. She'd reached out to him in the first place and that was a positive step. That gave him something to work with.

Will check in with Abby and get back to you. Tell Mason that I'll see him soon, okay?

I will.

Came the response. Then she sent Abby's phone number.

Dawson needed to think. Where could Abby be? It was possible that she was somewhere there was no cell coverage.

There were plenty of places to camp in and around Austin that were off the grid. School was about to start and Abby could be having one last hurrah.

Of course, Texas temperatures at this time of year could be brutal, and even she didn't go camping in August, it was generally ten degrees hotter in Austin than in North Texas. Okay, camping might be out of the question.

Melanie hadn't said it, but he knew that she was worried about the same conclusion Dawson had come to… the possibility that Sprigs had her.

But then wouldn't he make contact? Try to use her as a bargaining chip to get to Melanie? He would only take Abby to draw Melanie out. Right? That was the only thing that made sense.

What about Abby's friends? Didn't Melanie say something about a boyfriend? Maybe Dawson could start his search there. Surely someone knew where she was.

Dawson could grab his laptop and log on to her social media account to locate her pals as soon as he got to his parents' place. Then he could do some digging to see where she might be.

The rest of the car ride was quiet.

By the time Dawson returned to Mason Ridge, he'd had a chance to think through a couple of options at locating Abby. He had his folks take him to their house, since that was the last place he'd been before all this started.

What had begun as him wallowing in his own anguish, watching Melanie's parents' house across the street, had turned into a crazy eleven days.

He'd become a father and his entire life had been turned on its head.

And he'd do it all again if it meant meeting his child and seeing Melanie.

"The Dixons had a break-in recently, so I want both of you to exercise caution, okay?" Dawson said to his parents as they parked in the attached garage. He touched his mother's shoulder. "For you, that means staying in the garage with the engine running until the door closes behind you."

She nodded and offered a hopeful smile.

"It's going to take some time, but I'll do my best to move forward after what you've done," he said to her.

"None of this was supposed to happen this way," she

said, and she sounded sad. "I'm not making excuses, but I panicked when I realized what was going on and made a huge mistake."

There was more to it than that, because she'd had a thousand opportunities to tell him since then. "Is it Melanie you don't like?"

"It's not her exactly," his mother said. "She seems like a nice girl, and the two of you were so close growing up. In some ways I guess I felt like she'd taken you away from us after Bethany…"

Dawson started to defend Melanie, but his mom stopped him.

"We had so much grief that we shut down. That wasn't your fault or hers and I realize that now," she said. "When I found out she was pregnant I also realized that I couldn't go through that again."

"Melanie's pregnancy shouldn't have been about you, Mother."

"You're right," she said. "Too much of our life has been about me since Bethany."

When he really thought about it, Bethany's sickness had been about his mother. She'd been the grieving doctor who couldn't heal her own child. The depression she'd succumbed to afterward when she couldn't get out of bed had been about her, too. She hadn't thought of her husband or her son. And it had almost ruined their family.

They had been able to move forward and repair their relationships.

Dawson was an idiot. He shouldn't have doubted Melanie earlier. And as for her knowing him better than anyone else, she did. But she was wrong about one thing. If Mason had inherited the gene, Dawson could handle whatever came with it. He was a father. And being a loving parent meant putting his child's needs first.

Dawson shook his dad's hand. It had been his father who'd finally pulled the family up by their bootstraps. He loved his wife and he must have seen it as his job to protect her.

On some level, Dawson understood. His mother was strong on the outside but fragile when it came to inner strength.

Melanie could take care of herself. But that wouldn't stop Dawson from loving her and wanting to take care of her. The image of her standing in front of him with a shotgun leveled at his chest on the back porch the other day brought a smile to his face.

A woman like that wouldn't cave under any circumstance and especially one that involved her child.

Dawson excused himself, went inside and booted up his laptop. He checked Abby's social media page. So much for narrowing down her friends. She had 1480. No one had that many friends. He scrolled through her photos, hoping that he'd be able to figure out who her closest contacts were. Figuring out who she actually spent time with was his best hope of locating her.

He scanned her page for any posts that might signify where she was. There was nothing identifying her location. Normally, he'd be happy about the fact that she seemed to practice internet safety. Under the current circumstances, he was less than thrilled.

As expected, there were only a handful of people that she hung out with regularly according to her posts. Much to his good fortune, she'd identified them by placing tags on them with their names highlighted.

One of whom he was able to deduce must be Abby's roommate. Her name was Tabitha and he knew that they shared a house in Austin near campus.

Abby last posted three days ago. There was a pic of

her and a guy who wasn't tagged with a name. He was good-looking, athletic.

The pair looked cozy. This must be the new boyfriend.

Maybe Tabitha would know. Dawson fired off a private message asking her to call him with any information she had about Abby's whereabouts. He identified himself as a friend of Abby's sister and hoped Tabitha would get back in touch with him soon.

Being away from Melanie and Mason made Dawson feel empty inside. He missed the little whirlwind that was his son.

Dawson was too far away to ensure their safety and he had a bad feeling about Sprigs being so quiet. If the guy had been hurt in the crash—and what were the odds that he wasn't?—then he'd had enough time to heal and get some strength back.

The feds had planted a woman at Melanie's place, but they didn't seem to be getting any bites there.

Sprigs might have been a loner, but he was intelligent.

Dawson knew so little about the guy, and yet they'd grown up in the same town together. What if he made a few calls? Tried to get to know the guy a little better? Didn't he used to live off Maddox Street? That wasn't so far from where Dawson was now.

Time was ticking and Dawson wouldn't get to see Melanie or Mason again until this whole mess was sorted out.

His first call was to his buddy Ryan. Ryan's brother was in the same grade as Sprigs. Maybe he would know something about the guy's background.

Ryan picked up on the first ring. "Dawson, where are you?"

"How's Lisa?" Dawson tried to redirect.

"She's doing a lot better, thanks. She's been worried about Melanie, though," Ryan said.

"Melanie's with me."

Ryan relayed the information to Lisa.

She must've had a big reaction because the line went dead silent.

"Tell her that I know about Mason and it's okay," Dawson said. "We're working things out."

"Who's Mason?" Ryan asked.

"Long story. I'll tell you later," Dawson said. "In the meantime, I need to talk to Justin."

"What about?" Ryan had good reasons for being protective of his brother after they'd learned that the sheriff had been targeting him for years.

"It's about Melanie. Actually, it's about Jordan Sprigs."

"Whoa. Hold on there. Jordan Sprigs?" Ryan asked. "Beckett Alcorn's partner?"

"The very same one."

"What does Justin have to do with him?" Ryan asked, hesitant.

"Nothing personally. The two were in the same grade and I'm hoping that Justin can tell me something about the guy."

"Hold on. I'll conference him in right now," Ryan said.

Dawson's social media page made a ping noise. He had a message. He opened his laptop. Sure enough, there was a message from Tabitha.

Haven't seen Abby in two days. She didn't leave a note. It was weird. I'm at work but I'll call you later.

A heavy feeling pressed down on Dawson. He typed a thank-you along with his number as Justin came on the line.

Ryan let his brother know that Dawson was listening, and then asked Justin if he knew Jordan Sprigs.

"Not really," Justin said after exchanging greetings with Dawson. "He was strange, though."

"What kind of strange?" Dawson asked.

"At first we thought his mom was some kind of witch because she always wore plain dark clothes when she came to school to pick him up. She was a scary-looking woman, wild eyes and stringy hair. And she was strict." Justin paused, thinking. "I heard rumors about some of her punishments."

"Was it anything like what we went through with Dad?" Ryan asked.

"Nothing at all. What we went through was normal compared to what this crazy witch did. She was all religious but not in the 'have a glass of wine on Friday and then go to church on Sunday' way. I heard she used to routinely perform exorcisms when he disagreed with her or got a bad grade on a test. At first, I didn't take it seriously because I just thought kids were being cruel, but then I noticed how bad he looked some days and could tell he was being tender with his bruises."

"That sounds like a breeding ground for a psycho," Ryan interjected.

"Most of it could just be rumor and exaggeration. You know how that stuff takes on a life of its own. Couple it with the fact that the guy didn't act like a normal person and the rumor mill goes wild," Justin said. "There's someone who would know for certain what went on at the Sprigs house, and that's Peter Sheffield."

"The reporter?" Dawson asked.

"Yeah. He's right there in town." Justin paused, and Dawson could hear shouting in the background. "Girls, Daddy's on the phone."

Giggles followed by an apology came through next.

"Sorry. They have a knack for finding me anytime I'm

on my cell. It's like they have me on radar or something," Justin said, but he didn't sound the least bit upset. Maybe it was part of the parenting territory and he'd grown used to it.

Dawson thanked Justin for the lead. "I'm in Mason Ridge, so it'll be easy to track down Sheffield."

The guy wasn't popular among Dawson's friends because of the way he'd hounded Rebecca for a story about her brother.

They ended the conversation with Ryan saying they needed to get together again soon.

A quick call to the station and within five minutes Dawson had Sheffield on the line.

"I've been told by Justin Hughes that you knew Jordan Sprigs in high school," Dawson started after identifying himself.

"I don't know how well I knew him. We were in the same grade, as was Justin. Why? What's this about?" Sheffield asked.

"Do you know anything about his background?"

"Not much other than the fact that his father died when Jordan was still young and then his mother snapped," Sheffield said.

"How so?"

"She was weirdly religious to begin with, but when his father died she really jumped off the crazy ledge." Sheffield was being guarded with his responses and Dawson knew the guy was holding back. "Everyone in law enforcement is looking for him now that Alcorn rolled. What do you want with the guy?"

"My reasons for finding him are more of a personal nature." Dawson didn't have a good bargaining chip, so he figured honesty was his only hope.

Sheffield seemed to perk up. "What did he do to you?"

"He's fixated on someone who is important to me. And if I don't find him, he might kill her."

"And who is this person Sprigs is interested in?" Sheffield asked.

Again, honesty was the only course of action that made sense. If Dawson had another route, he'd gladly take it. "Melanie Dixon."

Sheffield made a strangled cough noise into the phone. "I thought she moved away a couple of years ago."

"She did. Mostly, to get away from him." That part wasn't one hundred percent truth, but Dawson figured he could fudge a little under the circumstances. And what was up with Sheffield's reaction?

"Where is she now?" he asked.

"She's being watched carefully," Dawson said.

"You don't know or you won't tell?" Sheffield asked, picking up on the nuisance of Dawson's language.

"I honestly don't know." That was true enough. And he cursed the fact that he didn't. "Will you tell me what you know about Sprigs?"

"Are you close to the investigation?" Sheffield seemed to be hesitating, deciding.

"Close enough to let you know the minute Sprigs is in custody." Dawson figured he'd throw that in for good measure. It remained to be seen if he could deliver on the promise, but a phone call once Sprigs was locked up wouldn't hurt anything.

"That's a deal." Sheffield seemed to perk up even more. "Sprigs and I weren't friends, but I had to stop over at his house to take homework to him once. He'd been out sick and we had the same homeroom teacher. He lived two blocks over, so I got stuck with the job. Inside, the place was strange. There was a wooden altar that had been constructed in the corner of the living room. I'd heard rumors that he had to kneel at that thing until the devil left him. I thought people were making it up. Never in my wildest dreams did I imagine that could be true."

"Sounds crazy."

"He'd come to class looking zonked and some of the kids said he literally had to sleep kneeling the entire time some nights. He did something wrong and he had to pray." Sheffield paused. "No one said for sure, but there were whispers of abuse. Spare the rod and all that."

"What couldn't be removed by praying she'd beat out of him?" Dawson asked.

"Something like that. You heard that rumor, too?"

"It was all around school," Dawson said. "I didn't take it seriously."

"Me neither. Until I saw that house," Sheffield said. "Then I believed all the rumors. The one about her locking him into a closet for days on end to pray. The one about her starving him so the devil wouldn't have anything to feed off of. And especially the one about her beating him with a pickax handle."

"Sounds like the experience left an impression on you," Dawson said. He could only imagine what it would be like to grow up in a twisted house like that.

"The craziest times apparently happened when she used the candles on him," Sheffield said.

That was the reason he liked to burn things.

"What about his mother? Did you see her? Is she still around? She could walk right past me on the street and I wouldn't know it," Dawson said.

"Yeah, I did before. A few years ago she moved them to a trailer on the outskirts of town."

Now it was Dawson's turn to perk up. "You have an address?"

"Not exactly, but there aren't many places out there. It's

where Old Saw Mill Road meets FM 46. Sits on a couple acres. There isn't much else out there."

"And what about her? What does she look like?" Dawson asked.

Sheffield blew out a breath. "I haven't seen her in years, but I remember that she was fairly attractive before. Homely because of the way she dressed, but she had nice features, you know. Her hair was long, blond and she had big brown doe eyes."

Just like Melanie.

Chapter Eighteen

Dawson thanked Sheffield and ended the call. Randall had to have known about Sprigs's mother and chose to keep that information to himself. The logical reason was that Randall wouldn't be able to share information about an ongoing investigation, and Dawson realized that on some level.

Of course, given that his family hung in the balance, it still burned through him to realize information sharing was mostly a one-way street.

Maybe Dawson could interview Sprigs's mother. Get a clue as to where her son might be hiding. He loaded his shotgun and tucked it away safely on the floorboard in the backseat of his SUV.

It took forty-five minutes to drive to the area Sheffield had mentioned. A few wrong turns later and he managed to find a trailer that looked as if it belonged on an episode of a cop show.

His phone buzzed, so he pulled off to the side of the drive where he could keep an eye on the front door of the trailer while he answered. His phone didn't recognize the number.

"Hello, this is Tabitha." She had that perky college coed voice.

"Thank you for calling. I'm a friend of Melanie's. She's

worried about her sister and asked me to help find Abby."
That was all the information Tabitha needed to make a
decision as to whether or not she should trust him.

"When you find her, tell her the rent is due," Tabitha
quipped. There wasn't a hint of worry in her voice. Maybe
Abby had disappeared before? "She forgot to leave a check
and I don't need this kind of stress to start off the semester."

"Will do." Dawson paused. "You have any idea where
she could've gone?"

"None. And she's not answering any of my calls."

"There's a guy in the photos online and her sister
thinks she has a new boyfriend," Dawson said.

"Oh, yeah. His name is Bradly. They've been spending a lot of time together lately. I should've called him
first," Tabitha said.

"Does Bradly have a last name?"

"I'm not sure. You know who would, though? Carlton.
Let me check with him and get back to you," she said.

"I'd like to hear from you as soon as you know."

"You don't think something's happened to her, do
you?" she asked, and it was the first time she sounded
truly alarmed.

"I hope not."

"She could be somewhere out of cell range, or there've
been a few times she forgot her charger." Tabitha's voice
rose the more she spoke. She was beginning to see the
possibilities that both Melanie and Dawson feared.

He hadn't intended to scare Abby's roommate. But
then, he needed some urgency on this, and that was one
way to get it.

Dawson ended the call and then phoned Randall.

Staring at the trailer, Dawson figured he'd better go in
armed with information.

"What do you know about Ruth Sprigs?" Dawson asked as soon as Randall answered.

"That she'd most likely do anything to cover for her son," Randall said. At least he didn't lie about it.

"So you interviewed her?"

"Yes. Her and everyone else I could find connected to her son." Randall's tone was matter-of-fact. "There's news out of Houston. Someone is watching the apartment and we think it might be him."

It was too early to hope, but if that was true then Sprigs couldn't be hiding out at his mother's trailer. Although that was probably too obvious anyway. "Is his mother involved in illegal activity?"

"No connection has been established," Randall said in a convincing tone.

"If I told you I was staring at her trailer, would you give me some advice?" Dawson figured it was now or never and he needed to know how concerned law enforcement was about her.

"Yes. Plenty. Are you alone right now?" Randall asked.

"Yes," Dawson said.

"Then get out of there."

"I've made it this far. I'm not turning back," Dawson said, and he meant it.

"Then wait. Let me send someone out there for backup," Randall said.

"You get anything out of her before?"

"No." Again, he was being honest.

"I might. I'm local and she might be more willing to talk to me."

"She's a few cards short of a deck," Randall said. "And I don't want you anywhere near that place."

"I might be able to help," Dawson said. "To end this once and for all."

"Let my people do their jobs."

Dawson understood Randall's position. It had been weeks since this whole ordeal began with Melanie and so much longer than that if they really went back to the beginning. What did anyone have to show for it?

Sure, Beckett Alcorn was in jail. At least for now. Wasn't it Randall who'd said it was only a matter of time before Alcorn's fancy lawyers got him out on some technicality? Stories like his littered the news.

Dawson couldn't risk it. His family was at stake.

"I gotta go," he said before ending the call to the background noise of Randall's protests.

The area was thickly wooded and the nearest major street was a good twenty minutes away. There was no way to sneak up because the road only led to one place, the trailer.

Even though the property consisted of several acres, there was a fence around the trailer, giving the impression of an enclosed front and backyard.

Dawson turned his SUV around and parked on the lane outside the fence. No one had opened the front door, which meant they were either content to watch him from the window or not home.

The trailer was old, the metal fence rusted. There was a beat-up tire tied to a tree in the side yard. It was the kind of place he expected to see a Rottweiler chained out front.

In fact, Dawson scanned the yard for animal feces as he breached the gate.

He took a deep breath and caught wind of something awful, a stench like rotting meat left out in 110 degree weather. The closer he stepped toward the trailer, the more pungent the odor. It was something worse than trash left to sour. There was something oddly sweet but overpowering about this scent. And it made him want to puke.

Dawson pulled his shirt over his nose and mouth to filter the air he breathed. It helped a little. He took the two makeshift wooden steps to the trailer in one stride and then knocked on the door.

There were no barking dogs and he sighed in relief. The last thing he needed was an encounter with a pit bull.

Then again, there was no noise at all.

He pressed his forehead to the glass, trying to get a look inside. The blinds were closed and with the bright sun to his back he caught a glare off the window.

The smell was about to double him over as he walked around to the back of the trailer. He hoped to see a metal trash barrel full of rotting garbage instead of what he most feared.

Melanie was fine, she was with Randall or one of his men. It was Abby he was worried about. And that was what prompted him to break the law and kick the back door open.

As soon as the door flew open, the stench cloaked him.

Dawson stumbled a step backward, tripping down the makeshift staircase and landing on his back. The wind knocked out of him.

Jumping to his feet, he curled his arm around his face, nose to the crook of his arm, to stave off the nauseating odor.

He gripped his cell in his other hand and called back the last number he'd phoned just as he glimpsed a female body slumped over in a plaid recliner. He couldn't get a good enough look at it to tell if it was Melanie's sister, and since he had no idea if the murderer was still around, he had no plans to run inside to check.

"There's been a murder," Dawson said.

"Get out of there," Randall said. "We're on our way."

Dawson jogged over to his SUV. It would be safe to

wait inside there and he needed a break from the overwhelming stench or he was about to toss his breakfast.

Even running the engine and turning the AC on high couldn't completely get rid of the smell that clung to his shirt like Louisiana humidity.

Staying alert, he waited for one of Randall's men to show.

Much to his surprise, the sedan that pulled in was driven by Randall. He parked next to Dawson and it looked as though he instructed Melanie to stay in the vehicle.

"We were the closest to you. I've alerted local law enforcement and they're on the way. We don't make a move until they get here," Randall said.

"She shouldn't be here," Dawson said to Randall as he exited the car and closed the door.

"We had a situation, so we had to transfer her to my vehicle," Randall said. "I couldn't leave you here alone or risk the crime scene being tampered with by the sheriff. Especially after learning about his relationship with the Alcorn family. This case has been mishandled dating back to the abductions fifteen years ago."

Dawson couldn't argue with that point. And he'd had his suspicions about Sheriff Brine's integrity along the way.

"We need to take a walk," Dawson said.

Randall followed to a spot where Dawson was sure Melanie couldn't overhear what he needed to tell the agent.

"Her sister is missing and I didn't get a good enough look at who was inside there to know if it was Abby," Dawson said.

"Based on the smell and the heat, this person has been

in there for a few days at least. I'm guessing there'll be significant decomposition given the circumstances."

"Meaning?" Dawson asked.

"Even if I walked inside right now, I might not be able to determine who it is."

"The body was too small to be a man's," Dawson said. "That much I could tell."

"Then we're dealing with a woman, his mother, or possibly a child," Randall replied.

Dawson's stomach churned as he thought about the possibilities. Given Sprigs's history, it could be either. Based on the size, Dawson's money was on a female.

"We'll bring in a team to analyze the crime scene," Randall said. "It'll take a little while to process. You leave messages with her sister?"

Dawson nodded.

"Then let's hope she calls back soon."

"She's been missing for three days." Dawson moved to the parked sedan. The door opened and Melanie climbed out, holding Mason against her chest.

"What is that smell?" she asked, wrinkling her nose.

"You might want to stay inside with Mason and keep the AC on," Dawson said, leaning in to kiss Mason's forehead and then Melanie's before urging them back inside. He didn't want to get too close while he had the dead body stench all over him.

"Dada." Mason's face lit up.

"I'm here, buddy." He looked at Melanie. "And I'm not going anywhere."

She squeezed his arm. "We need to talk."

"We will. Soon." He had no intention of letting her disappear again without knowing how he really felt about her and Mason.

"Did you find out anything about Abby?" she asked.

"Her roommate is trying to reach Bradly?"

"That's a good sign. She's done this before when she meets someone," Melanie said, looking a little relieved.

"She's planning to call me back here in a few minutes," he said. He hoped that was all there was to it. Abby had met a new guy and had fallen off the radar. If that was true then Tabitha could be calling back with good news soon.

Melanie smiled tentatively, nodding as she climbed inside the cab.

He closed the door and then instructed her to lock it, feeling a small sense of relief when he heard sirens in the distance.

By the time he turned around, Randall was on the phone. Good. Maybe there'd be an update about when other law enforcement officers would be there and Randall could take Melanie far away. Dawson had a bad feeling about her being anywhere near this place, and God forbid her sister be the one inside that trailer. The two were close and Dawson knew it would destroy Melanie if anything had happened to Abby.

The most likely scenario was that the body in there belonged to Sprigs's mother. And there was a less likely possibility that it was a child. In general, Sprigs and Alcorn took younger kids, three years old and younger. The only cases of older children being taken had to do with Kramer's greediness and nothing to do with the operation.

"There's a problem," Randall said to Dawson as soon as he ended the call.

Dawson didn't like the sound of that. He'd been catching the occasional whiff of something he couldn't immediately identify. He wrote it off as whatever was in that trailer.

"Emergency vehicles can't get through."

When he really thought about it, the sirens hadn't moved closer in the past few seconds. "What's going on? Someone blocking the road?"

"Not someone, some*thing*." Randall looked Dawson directly in the eye. "Fire."

The opening to the lane was far away and there were enough trees around to block their vision. Plus, the stench would mask the smoke, at least for a while.

And that meant one thing... Sprigs was there.

Dawson marched over to his SUV and pulled out his shotgun. "We'll have a better chance of getting out of here alive if we take my SUV."

"There's only one road in and out," Randall said.

"Then we'll have to make our own way out the back," Dawson countered. He ushered Melanie and Mason out of the sedan and grabbed the car seat with his free hand. He locked it dead center in his backseat.

Randall was on the phone again. "They're battling the blaze as they look for a way out for us through satellite pictures of the property."

"Being here isn't going to help us. I can get us through that clearing." Dawson pointed to a place opposite the entrance. "Find out where that'll take us, because we're not staying here. That's exactly what he wants and he could be anywhere."

The land was fairly flat in this part of North Texas, and that made traversing the terrain a bit easier as Dawson navigated as far away from the trailer as possible. The main problem was trees. They were getting closer together and Randall had already warned that there was a creek coming up that would block their path. Being inside the SUV offered some shelter and Dawson didn't like the idea of leaving its safety.

Sprigs would most likely know the woods, and Dawson

couldn't help noting that he was positioning them away from anyone who could help them.

Randall got another phone call, which he put on speaker.

"I've got more bad news. A couple more fires have been set. One is directly in the way of the new path." The voice belonged to Andy.

"Where are you?" Randall asked.

"We're doing our best to set a perimeter, but this is a lot of acreage to cover," Andy said.

Dawson didn't say what he was thinking out loud. This was the perfect setup for Sprigs. He was encasing them with fire. The question remaining was whether or not he'd stay inside the circle or bolt so he could find a place to watch them burn.

Dawson hit the brake at the edge of the creek and the SUV lurched forward. They couldn't go back. Trees to the left and right were too thick to drive through. As much as he hadn't wanted to consider the possibility, they had no choice but to get out on foot.

"How about following the water?" Dawson asked. Could they allow the creek to lead them out of there? As soon as he opened his window, the smell of smoke carried in on the breeze. The crackle of fire meant that it was close.

Well, Sprigs didn't get to orchestrate the perfect murder on Dawson's watch.

Randall took the call off speaker. He listened before ending the call, closing his eyes and leaning his head back on the headrest. "The blaze is all around us. We're not getting out."

"What about a chopper?" Dawson asked.

"By the time one gets here, it'll be too late. The dry

conditions have the fire moving too swiftly," Randall supplied.

"This is all happening too fast," Dawson said. "There's no way he's setting these fires by himself."

"The officers found a rig set up at the opening of the drive. He wired this place before and he's been watching," Randall said.

Which meant Sprigs might not even be there. He could be setting these fires using a remote. Dammit. Anger burst through Dawson's chest.

He had no plans to roll over for that son of a bitch and allow the fire to consume everyone he loved.

"If we follow the water source, there might be a way to get out," Dawson said.

"Everyone out. Grab the diaper bag," Randall instructed.

Melanie had been quiet up to now. She got out of the vehicle and held Mason to her chest. "Dawson, I'm really sorry about—"

"We'll have time to talk about it later," he said, his words meant to reassure her. No way was he allowing her to give up.

Randall pulled up the GPS on his phone. "Looks like the creek runs northwest. If we follow it long enough, we might be able to make it to FM 33."

"Good. That's the route we'll take. I have emergency supplies in my trunk." Dawson moved to the back of his SUV and retrieved his backpack.

He came back to the group and kissed Melanie's forehead.

"We're going to get out of here," he whispered.

Chapter Nineteen

Dawson led them along the creek for a good twenty minutes before he hit a thick wall of smoke.

Moving forward was no longer an option. Mason's lungs wouldn't be able to take much more.

A wall of fire blocked any chance of moving west, so Dawson had no choice but to circle back. They were beginning to walk into fire now. It was all around them.

Dawson didn't want to separate from the creek, but there would be no choice soon.

A fiery branch fell from above. Thick smoke was beginning to make Mason cough. And they were starting to walk in circles.

And then they heard it. A man's voice. A distorted laugh from the south. Sprigs.

"Go ahead, run," Randall said. "I'll slow him down."

Dawson hesitated at first, but Randall insisted. Even though Dawson wanted to stay back to help the agent, there was no way he would send Melanie ahead on her own.

Grabbing Melanie's hand, Dawson ran until a fallen tree blocked the trail, forcing him to move them east again.

"Let's stop here and rest." Dawson needed to check his phone to see if Randall had tried to reach them.

Besides, Melanie was out of breath and she needed a minute before he pushed them to keep moving again. There was a bottle of water in his emergency pack. He took it out and handed it to her.

She plopped down on the ground with Mason in her lap. He'd been such a good boy so far, taking in all the strange sights and sounds, no doubt thinking they were on a grand adventure.

On Dawson's phone was a text from Tabitha.

Abby just called. Said she'll check in with her sister to-night.

"Abby's safe. Her roommate just sent a message saying that she's been hanging out at her new boyfriend's place before the semester started and had lost her charger." At least he was able to give Melanie good news for a change.

"Once I'm finished with you, your sister will join you in hell," Sprigs said from behind them a good twenty-five feet away.

Dawson rounded on Sprigs, blocking his view of Melanie. The movement must've startled Mason, because he started crying.

"Randall?" Dawson shouted.

"He can't help you," Sprigs said, agitated.

"You're not taking her, Sprigs," Dawson said.

Sprigs fired a shot. Dawson grabbed his chest, and then he took a few steps back before falling to the ground. He felt wet and cold. He didn't move because for Sprigs to get to Melanie he'd have to run right past Dawson.

She let out a scream and, best Dawson could tell, tore off in the direction opposite Sprigs.

Sprigs cursed and Dawson could hear footsteps racing toward him. He had to time it just right…

When he caught sight of a tennis shoe six inches from his head, he twisted to his side, ignoring the shooting pain in his chest, and grabbed Sprigs by the ankle.

Caught off guard, Sprigs face-planted in the dirt next to Dawson. Another shot fired and Dawson prayed the stray bullet didn't hit Melanie or Mason.

"Run, Melanie," he shouted.

"Come back or I'll kill him," Sprigs threatened.

"Like hell you will. And if by some miracle you do, then I'm taking you with me." Dawson wrestled for control of the gun.

Sprigs was one of those wiry guys, surprisingly strong for his size. If Dawson was full strength, there'd be no doubt who would come out on top. As it was, he was losing a lot of blood.

Dawson wriggled his arm free, spun around until he was sitting on Sprigs's chest and punched him.

Sprigs's nose squirted blood as he fought back, jabbing Dawson where he'd been shot.

Blinding pain nearly caused Dawson to pass out, but he fought to stay conscious. He needed to give Melanie more time to get far away and he needed to make sure Sprigs would never bother her again.

Dawson highly doubted he'd get out of these woods alive given his condition and the lack of medical support. By the time he made it out of there, he would bleed out.

So he reared back and punched Sprigs one more time, knocking him unconscious.

Somewhere in the back of his mind, he heard Mason crying.

He pushed himself off Sprigs and rolled onto his back again, staring up at the canopy of trees. The crackle of the fire was getting even closer and it wouldn't be long before the smoke lulled him into a permanent sleep.

Melanie was fine. Mason was alive. That was all that mattered.

The crying grew louder and before Dawson could sit properly, he heard footsteps.

No. No. No.

Melanie was supposed to run far away. She was smart enough to realize that.

Reality dawned.

That meant one thing. She was trapped, too.

"Melanie," Dawson called out.

The footsteps came closer as Dawson pushed himself up to his feet, leaning against a tree for support.

"I'm here," she said, and her voice was like an angel's.

Dawson blinked and saw two blurry figures running toward him. One was holding Mason.

"Melanie, get out of here," he said.

"I'm not leaving you, Dawson," she said, putting his arm around her shoulder.

"Dada," Mason said, leaning toward Dawson. He wanted to hold his son more than he wanted to breathe.

"What are you doing? Now we'll all die," Dawson whispered to Melanie.

"I found a tunnel," she said. "It's how he got to us."

Randall was standing over a still-woozy Sprigs, his foot planted on Sprigs's back.

"Leave him," Dawson said as Melanie took Mason.

"Oh, no. This scumbag's going with us. Dying is too good for this jerk. He's got a lifetime date in a jail cell," Randall said as he cuffed the criminal.

"You won't keep me locked behind bars for long," Sprigs snarled.

"Yes. I will. And you know how I know you're going to have a long and painful life in prison?" Randall said, pulling Sprigs to his feet. "Because you're going to be very popular there. All those burly men in for life without parole are going to enjoy spending quality time with you. So you better plan to start talking and give up everyone you've been working with, every route you've set up."

Melanie led them through a tunnel that had been built as a water runoff in case the creek flooded.

There were medical personnel waiting on the scene as soon as they broke through to the other side onto the farm road.

Dawson dropped to his knees, exhausted.

"I love you, Melanie. I want to be a real family with you and Mason. Marry me and make me the happiest man alive," he said as EMTs flanked him and his eyes closed.

"THE SURGERY WENT WELL," Dr. Granger said, still wearing his surgical scrubs.

"That's good news," Melanie said. She'd been waiting, pacing for a solid eight hours.

Andy had been kind enough to offer to stay with her and Mason. He'd said he could use the practice entertaining a toddler. And he'd been great. Watching Mason with Andy made her miss Dawson all that much more.

"You can go in and see him now," the doctor said. "He's in room 210."

Melanie thanked him and walked as fast as she could without running.

She looked at Dawson, lying in bed with machines beeping and tubes coming out of him, and her heart stuttered.

All she could do was pull up a chair by his side and wait for him to open his eyes.

It took another three hours.

He blinked his eyes open and said something she couldn't understand.

"Hey, there, stranger," she replied. "It's okay." She squeezed his hand. "You don't have to talk right now."

He let go of hers and pointed toward the plastic cup of water.

"You're thirsty?" she asked.

He nodded.

She helped him position himself up so he could take a few sips. He blinked a couple of times and really looked at her.

"You didn't answer my question," he said clearly this time.

She looked around. "What? I already gave you some water. Do you want more?"

He shook his head like he was shaking out of a fog and then kissed her hand.

"I asked you to marry me," he said.

Melanie's heart filled with joy.

"Yes, Dawson, I will marry you."

"I love you, Melanie. I always have." He kissed her hand again.

"Confession?" she asked.

He nodded.

"It's you. It's always been you. I have wanted to marry you since we were ten years old and sat on the old stoop together." She didn't stop the tears from streaming down her face. "I have always loved you, Dawson."

Dawson pulled her toward him for a hug, kissing her on her forehead, her eyes, her nose, before pressing his lips to hers in a slow, sweet kiss.

He thumbed away her tears. "I understand what you were saying about Mason before and not needing to know. We don't have to get him tested."

"You were right, Dawson. I was scared before. I'm not

when you're with me. I think we need answers and I'm ready to face whatever life brings our way."

"No matter what happens, I'll be right beside you, loving you with everything that I am. We'll make it through this life together, making our own mistakes, and you'll never be alone again."

"I love you," was all she could manage to say through her tears.

Epilogue

"Don't you think it's a little too cold outside to fire up the grill?" Melanie asked Dawson.

When it came to weather this time of year in Texas, anything was possible.

"It'll be fine," Dawson reassured her. "Besides, this seems like a steak-on-the-grill kind of announcement."

She laughed as their friends began arriving couple by couple.

Everyone already knew to come around back, where she was playing with Mason on his new swing set.

Maribel barreled around the side of the house and Mason squealed the second he saw her.

Melanie helped him out of his swing. He ran across the yard until he and Maribel locked in embrace. They crashed into each other, fell down and rolled around laughing. Dylan and Samantha followed. And then Rebecca and Brody arrived, followed by Lisa and Ryan.

It was reassuring to see how much Mason loved other children.

The town had been through so much last summer and yet everyone seemed to bounce back.

There was a renewed feeling of life and a sense of relief after both Alcorn and Sprigs had been convicted and the sheriff had been removed from office, facing corruption charges. The rest of the ring had been busted and children played safely in their yards again.

Times were changing and Mason Ridge was beginning to feel the way it used to when they were all innocent kids. Or maybe there was a new wave of innocence breathing life into the place as a heavy cloud had lifted.

Alice and Jack walked around the corner and Melanie waved to them.

"What's going on?" Dawson asked, clearly surprised to see them.

"I invited them," Melanie said. She pushed herself up on her tiptoes and kissed her husband. "They deserve to know, too."

Bonds were still tentative, but Melanie wanted to make an effort.

Her own parents had pulled up in their RV an hour ago. Abby's semester was in full swing, so she couldn't make it to the party. Melanie had promised to fill her sister in on everything that went on later.

"I'll go wake your folks," Dawson said, patting Melanie's backside.

He returned with them five minutes later.

The sun cast a bright orange glow in the sky. Everyone gathered around the long wooden table.

Melanie couldn't think of a better night to share the news.

Dawson made sure everyone had a drink before taking his spot next to Melanie.

"We're glad everyone could make it tonight," he began. "We have a special announcement to make and we wanted our friends and family to be the first to know."

Friends raised their glasses in salute.

"Come here, buddy," Dawson said to Mason. "You want to tell everyone the good news?"

Mason grinned and nodded. He pointed to Melanie's stomach and said, "Baby."

Cheers rang out and hugs abounded.

Mason was right. There was a baby coming early next summer. Doctors had reassured them that both of their children were fine.

And Mason would live a long and healthy life with his little sister.

* * * * *

Read on for an excerpt from
HARD RAIN
The next installment in
New York Times *bestselling author*
B.J. Daniels's series
THE MONTANA HAMILTONS.

When Brody McTavish sees Harper Hamilton's runaway
horse galloping across the pastures, he does what any
good cowboy would do—gives chase and rescues her. But
they soon have bigger problems when they make a grue-
some discovery—human remains that will dredge up old
Hamilton family mysteries...and bring about a scandal
that could threaten all Harper's loved ones.

CHAPTER ONE

Thunder cracked overhead in a piercing boom that rattled the windows. As she huddled in the darkness, rain pelted down in angry drenching waves. Lightning again lit the sky in a blinding flash that burned in her mind the image before her.

In that instant, she saw him crossing the field carrying the shovel, his head down, rain pouring off his black Stetson. It was done.

Dark clouds blanketed the hillside. Through the driving rain, she watched him come toward her, telling herself she could live with what she'd done. But she feared he could not. And that could be a problem.

BRODY MCTAVISH HEARD the screams only seconds before he heard the roar of hooves headed in his direction. Shoving back his cowboy hat, he looked up from the fence he'd been mending to see a woman on a horse riding at breakneck speed toward him.

Harper Hamilton. He'd heard that she'd recently returned after being away at college. Which meant it could have been years since she'd been on a horse. He was already grabbing for his horse's reins and swinging up in the saddle.

Runaway horse.

He'd been on a runaway horse when he was a kid. He remembered how terrifying it had been. With that many pounds of horseflesh running at such a deadly speed, he prayed hard she could hang on.

He had to hand it to Harper. She hadn't been unseated. At least not yet.

Harper, yards away on a large bay, screamed. He spurred his horse to catch her and as he raced up beside her, her blue eyes were wide with alarm.

Acting quickly, he looped an arm around her, dragged her off the horse and reined in. His horse came to a stop in a cloud of dust. Her horse kept going, disappearing into the foothill pines ahead.

Brody let Harper slip to the ground next to his horse. The minute her feet touched earth, she started screaming again as if all the wind had been knocked out of her when he'd grabbed her but was back now.

"You're all right," he said, swinging out of the saddle and stepping to her to try to calm her.

She spun on him, leading with her fist, and caught him in the jaw. He staggered back more from surprise than the actual blow, but the woman had a pretty darned good right hook.

He stared at her in confusion. "What the devil was that about?"

Picking up a baseball-sized rock, she brandished it as she took a few steps back from him, all the time glancing around, seeming either to expect more men to come out of the foothills, or looking for a larger weapon.

Had the woman hit her head? He spoke as calmly as he would to a skittish horse—or a crazy woman. "Calm down. I know you're scared. But you're all right now." It had only been a few months since the two of them were attendants at her sister Bo's wedding, not that they hadn't known each other for years.

She peered under the brim of his hat as if only then

taking a good look at him. "Brody McTavish?" She stared at him as if in shock. "Have you lost your mind?"

Brody frowned, since this hadn't been the reaction he'd expected. "Ah, correct me if I'm wrong," he said, rubbing his jaw. "But I don't think this is the way most women would react after a man saves her life."

"You think you just saved my life?" Her voice rose in amazement.

"You were *screaming* like either a woman in trouble or one who has lost her senses. I assumed, as any sane person would, that your horse had run away with you. No need to thank me," he said sarcastically.

"Thank you? For scaring me half to death?" She dropped the rock and dusted the dirt off her hand onto her jeans. "And for the record, I wasn't *screaming*. I was… expressing myself."

"Expressing yourself at the top of your lungs?"

Harper jammed her hands on her hips and thrust out her adorable chin. He recalled her sister's wedding back at Christmastime. While both attendants, they hadn't shared more than a few words. Nor had he gotten a chance to dance with her. His own fault. He hadn't wanted to get in line with all her young suitors.

"It was a beautiful morning," she said haughtily. "I hadn't been on a horse in a long time and it felt so good that I couldn't resist expressing it." She looked embarrassed but clearly wasn't about to admit it. "Do you have a problem with that?"

"Nope. But when I see a woman riding like a wild person, screaming her head off, I'm going to assume she's in trouble and needs some help. My mistake." Didn't she know how dangerous it was riding like that out here? If her horse had stepped into a gopher hole… A lecture came to his lips, but he clamped his mouth shut. "You have a nice day, Miss Hamilton." He tipped his hat, grabbed up his reins and started to walk back toward his property.

"You're just going to walk away?" she demanded to his back.

"Since you aren't in need of *my* help…" he said over his shoulder.

"I thought you would at least help me retrieve my horse."

He stopped and mumbled under this breath, "If your horse has any sense he'll keep going."

"I beg your pardon?"

Brody took a breath and turned to face her again.

Her blond hair shone in the morning sunlight, her blue eyes wide and filled with devilment. He recalled the girl she'd been. Feisty was an understatement. While nothing had changed as far as that went, she was definitely no longer a girl. He would have had to be blind not to notice the way she filled out her jeans and Western shirt.

She shifted her boots in the dust. "I'd appreciate it if you would help me find my horse."

"By all means let me help you find your horse then. As you said, it's the least I can do. Would you care to ride…*Miss Hamilton*?" He motioned to his horse, glad he hadn't called her *Princess*, even though it had been on the tip of his tongue.

Looking chastised, she shook her head. "And, please, my name is—"

"Harper. I know."

"Glad you didn't mistake me for my twin." She sounded more than a little surprised. "Not even my own father can tell us apart at times."

He could feel her looking at him, studying him like a bug under a microscope. He wondered what she'd majored in at college. Nothing useful, he would bet.

"Thank you for helping me find my horse," she said into the silence that fell between them. "I really don't want to be left out here on foot if my horse has returned to the barn."

He thought the walk might do her some good but was smart enough not to voice it. "The last I saw of your mare she was headed up into the foothills. I would imagine that's where we'll find her, next to the creek."

She glanced up at him. "I apologize for hitting you." When he said nothing, she continued. "With everything that's been going on in my family, I thought you were... Anyway, I'm sorry that I hit you and that I misunderstood your concern." He could hear in her voice how hard that apology was for her.

And, he had to admit, her family had recently definitely been through a lot. The family had seemed to be under attack since her father, Senator Buckmaster Hamilton, had announced he would be running for president. Three of her sisters had been threatened. Not to mention the mother she'd believed dead had returned out of the blue after twenty-two years—and her stepmother had been killed in a car accident. It was as if tragedy was tracking that family.

"Apology accepted," he said as he picked up her cowboy hat from the dust and handed it to her.

As they walked toward sun-bleached cliffs and shimmering green pines, he mentally kicked himself. He'd had a crush on Harper—from a distance, of course—for years, waiting for her to grow up, and now that she finally had and he'd managed to get her attention, he couldn't imagine a worse encounter.

Not that he wasn't knocked to his knees by her crooked smile or the way she had of cocking her head when she was considering something. Not to mention the endless blue of her wide-eyed innocence—all things he'd noticed from the first time he'd laid eyes on her. He smiled to himself, remembering the first time he'd seen her. She'd just been a freckle-faced kid.

Somehow, he'd thought… She'd be grown up and one day… He told himself someday he and Harper would have a good laugh over this, before he mentally kicked himself.

And to think he thought he'd rescued the woman of his dreams—until she'd hit him.

BRODY MCTAVISH. HARPER grimaced in embarrassment. She'd been half in love with him as far back as she could remember. Not that he had looked twice at her. He'd been the handsome rowdy teen she used to spy on from a distance. She'd been just a girl, much too young for him. But Brody had come to parties her older sisters had put on at the ranch. She and Cassidy were too young to attend and were always sent up to bed, but Harper often sneaked down when everyone else, including her twin, thought she was asleep.

Several times Brody had caught her watching, and she'd thought for sure he would snitch on her, but he hadn't. Instead, he'd given her a grin and covered for her. Her nine-year-old heart had beat like a jackhammer in her chest at just the thought of that grin.

She'd seen Brody a few times after that, but only in passing. He'd graduated from high school and gone off to college before coming back to the ranch. She'd been busy herself, getting an education, traveling, experiencing life away from Montana. When she'd heard that her sister Bo was dating Jace Calder, she'd wondered if he and Brody were still best friends.

It wasn't until the wedding that she got to see him again. She hadn't been surprised to find that he was still handsome, still had that same self-deprecating grin, still made her now grown-up heart beat a little faster. She'd waited at the wedding reception for him to ask her to dance since they were both attendants, but he hadn't. She'd told herself that he probably still saw her as a child, given the difference in their ages.

Glancing over at him now, she didn't even want to consider what he must think of her after this. Not that she cared, she told herself, lifting her head and pretending it didn't matter. He probably didn't even remember the secret they had shared when she was a girl.

As they walked, though, she couldn't help studying him out of the corner of her eye. Earlier, she hadn't appreciated how strong he was. Now that she knew he wasn't some predator who had been trying to abduct her—something she'd been warned about since she was the daughter of a wealthy rancher and US senator—she took in his muscled body along with the chiseled features of his handsome face in the shade of his straw cowboy hat.

No matter what he said, he hadn't accepted her apology. He was still angry with her. She'd given him her best smile when he'd returned her hat from the ground and all she'd gotten was a grunt. Her smile was all it usually took with most men. But Brody wasn't most men. Wasn't that why she'd never been able to forget him?

"I feel as if we have gotten off on the wrong foot," she said, trying to make amends.

Another grunt without even looking at her.

"My fault entirely," she said, although she didn't really believe that was true and hoped he would agree.

But he said nothing, nor would he even look at her. He was starting to irritate her. She was doing her best to make up for the misunderstanding, but the stubborn man wasn't giving her an inch.

"You can't just keep ignoring me," she snapped, digging in her boot heels as she stopped shy of the pine-covered hillside. "Have you even heard a word I've said? If you don't look at me right this minute, Brody McTavish, I'm going to—"

He swung on her. Had she not been standing flat-footed she would have stumbled back. Instead, she was rooted to the ground as suddenly he was in her face. "I've *been* listening to you and I've *been* looking at you for years," he said, his voice deep and thick with emotion. "I've *been* waiting for you to grow up." His voice faltered as he dropped his horse's reins. "Because I've been wanting to do this since you were sixteen."

Grabbing her, he pulled her against his rock-hard body. His mouth dropped to hers. Her lips parted of their own accord, just as her arms wrapped around his neck. Her heart hammered against her ribs as he deepened the kiss and she heard herself moan.

The sudden high-pitched whinny of a horse only yards away brought them both out of the kiss in one startled movement. Turning, she could see her horse in the trees. Her first thought was that the mare had gotten into a hunter's snare, because the whinny was one of pain—or alarm.

Brody grabbed her arm as she started past him to see what was wrong with her horse. "I think you should wait here," he said, letting go of her arm as he took off toward the pines.

"My horse—"

"Stay here," he said more sternly over his shoulder.

Still stunned by the kiss and anxious about her horse, she set off after him. The ground was soft under her feet. She saw where fresh soil had washed down through the pines, forming a dark, muddy gully.

Her horse was partway up the hillside near where the rain a few nights ago had loosened the soil and washed it down the hillside. As Brody approached, the mare snorted and crow-hopped away a few feet.

"She's afraid of you," she called to his retreating backside. She could hear him speaking softly to the horse as he approached. She followed, although she was no match for his long legs.

An eerie quiet fell over the hillside as she stepped into the shadowed pines. She slowed, frowning as she finally got a good look at her horse. The mare didn't seem to be hurt and yet Harper had never seen her act like this before.

"I thought I told you to stay back," Brody said as she came up behind him. "You've never been good at following orders, have you?"

So he did remember her sneaking downstairs at her sisters' parties. She felt a bump of excitement at that news, but it was quickly doused. Past him, she saw that her horse's eyes were wild. The mare snorted again, stomped the ground and shied away to move a few yards back from them and the gully.

"What is wrong with her?" Harper demanded, afraid it was something she had done.

"She's reacting to what the hard rain dislodged and sent down the hillside in an avalanche of mud," Brody snapped. What was he talking about? As she started to step past him to get a look, he put a hand out to stop her. "Harper, you don't want to see this."

She *did* want to see whatever it was and resented him telling her she didn't. Protective was one thing, but the man was being ridiculous. She'd been raised on a ranch. She'd seen her share of dead animals, if that was what it was. She stepped around him, determined to see what the storm had exposed.

At first all she saw were old, grimy, weathered boards that looked like part of a large wooden box. Then she saw what must have been inside the container before it had washed down the slope and broken open.

Her pulse jumped at the sight, her mind telling her she wasn't seeing what her eyes told her she saw. *"What is that?"* she whispered into the already unnerving quiet as she took a step back.

"From the clothing and long hair, I'd say it was the mummified body of a woman who, until recently, had been buried up on that hillside."

Find out what happens next in
HARD RAIN by New York Times
bestselling author B.J. Daniels.
Available now wherever
HQN Books and ebooks are sold.
www.Harlequin.com

INTRIGUE

Available April 19, 2016

#1635 THE MARSHAL'S JUSTICE
Appaloosa Pass Ranch • by Delores Fossen
Despite the bad blood between marshal Chase Crockett and his former criminal informant, April Landis, he'll do whatever it takes to protect her from murderous thugs—and rescue their newborn daughter.

#1636 ALLEGIANCES
The Battling McGuire Boys • by Cynthia Eden
In order to save his ex-wife, Celia, PI Sully McGuire is forced to resurrect old demons. New dangers—and dormant desires—bring Sully and Celia close... and old enemies even closer.

#1637 ROPING RAY McCULLEN
The Heroes of Horseshoe Creek • by Rita Herron
PI Ray McCullen finds himself willing to do anything to keep social worker Scarlet Lovett safe from a mysterious threat. The only way to do that is to keep her by his side and make her a McCullen.

#1638 URGENT PURSUIT
Return to Ravesville • by Beverly Long
DEA agent Bray Hollister will risk everything to rescue ex-love Summer Wright's daughter. His job. His life. Even a second chance with the woman who was never far from his heart.

#1639 TRIBAL LAW
Apache Protectors • by Jenna Kernan
Tribal police chief Gabe Cosen is dedicated to the law—until his former fiancée, Selena Dosela, is forced into trafficking for a Mexican drug cartel. Now Gabe must choose between enforcing the law or protecting the woman he loves.

#1640 SMOKE AND ASHES • by Danica Winters
When Heather Sampson's world erupts into flames at the hands of a serial arsonist, she turns to Kevin Jensen, the sexy fire inspector next door, for help. Can he be her hero, or will she fall victim to her past?

HICNM0416

INTRIGUE

Read on for a sneak peek at ALLEGIANCES,
the conclusion of THE BATTLING McGUIRE BOYS
by New York Times bestselling author
Cynthia Eden

*In order to save his ex-wife, Celia, PI Sullivan McGuire
is forced to resurrect old demons. New dangers—and
dormant desires—bring Sully and Celia close…and old
enemies even closer.*

"Hello, Sullivan."

At that low, husky voice—a voice Sullivan had
heard far too many times in his dreams—his head
whipped up. He blinked, sure that he had to be imagining
the figure standing in his office doorway. He even shook
his head, as if that small movement could somehow make
the woman before him vanish.

Only she didn't vanish.

She laughed, and the small movement made her short
red hair brush lightly against her delicate jaw. "No,
sorry, you can't blink or even wish me away. I'm here."
Celia James stepped inside and shut the door behind her.

He rose to his feet in a quick rush. "I wouldn't wish
you away." Just the opposite. His voice had sounded too
gruff, so he cleared his throat. He didn't want to scare
her away, not when he had such plans for her. *And she's
actually here. Close enough to touch.* "Should you…
should you be here? You were hurt—"

Celia waved that injury away with a flick of her hand.

"A flesh wound. I've had worse." Sadness flickered in her eyes. "It's Elizabeth who took the direct hit. I was afraid for a while…but I heard she's better now."

He nodded and crept closer to her. Elizabeth Snow was the woman his brother Mac—MacKenzie—intended to marry as fast as humanly possible. Elizabeth was also the woman who'd been shot recently—when she faced off against a killer who'd been determined to put Elizabeth in the ground.

Only Elizabeth hadn't died, and that particular case… it had brought Celia back into Sullivan's life.

Now I can't let her leave.

He schooled his expression as he said, "She's out at the ranch. And I'm sure Mac is about to drive her crazy." He was absolutely certain of that fact. "I think his protective instincts kicked into overdrive." *So did mine. When I saw you on the ground…*

"I came to make you a deal," Celia said as she took a step toward him.

His head tilted to the side as he studied her. "A deal?" Now he was curious. Celia wasn't exactly the type to make deals. She was the type to keep secrets. The type to always get the job done, no matter what.

During Sullivan's very brief stint with the CIA, he'd met the lovely Celia.

And he'd fallen hard for her.

Until I thought she'd betrayed me.

Find out what happens in ALLEGIANCES by New York Times bestselling author Cynthia Eden.

Available May 2016 wherever Harlequin® Intrigue books and ebooks are sold.
www.Harlequin.com

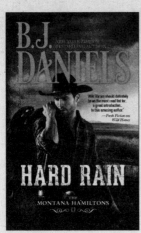

HARLEQUIN®

A *Romance* FOR EVERY MOOD™

JUST CAN'T GET ENOUGH?

Join our social communities
and talk to us online.

You will have access to the latest
news on upcoming titles and special
promotions, but most importantly,
you can talk to other fans about your
favorite Harlequin reads.

Harlequin.com/Community

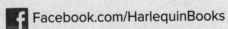

Facebook.com/HarlequinBooks

Twitter.com/HarlequinBooks

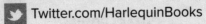

Pinterest.com/HarlequinBooks